DECEPTION

BY

BARBARA WARREN

DECEPTION WRITTEN BY BARBARA WARREN
Published by Lighthouse Publishing of the Carolinas
2333 Barton Oaks Dr., Raleigh, NC, 27614

ISBN: 978-1-938499-78-4
Copyright © 2013 by Barbara Warren
Cover design by Ken Raney: www.kenraney.com
Book design by Kate Irwin: www.kateinc.com

Available in print from your local bookstore, online, or from the publisher at:
www.lighthousepublishingofthecarolinas.com

Library of Congress Cataloging-in-Publication Data
Barbara Warren
Deception / Barbara Warren 1st ed.

Printed in the United States of America

Lighthouse Publishing
of the Carolinas
www.lighthousepublishingofthecarolinas.com

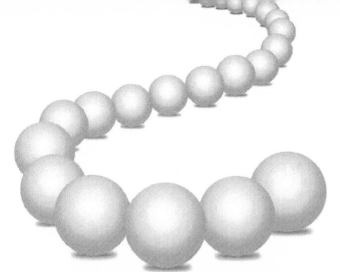

PROLOGUE

Tessie whimpered. "I want my Momma."

The skinny woman with a mop of kinky blond hair slapped her arm. "Don't let me hear any more of that whining."

The car sped down the street.

Tessie crawled toward her big sister. Rhona wrapped arms around her, whispering in her ear. "It's all right, Tessie. Daddy will come after us. Don't cry."

The woman hit Tessie on the cheek. "Shut your mouth. I ain't listening to that racket."

"Now, Aggie," said the man. "Just think of all that cash we'll be getting. All them new clothes you can buy. We'll live like royalty."

"If we don't get caught. I still say this was a fool's trick, Morris. We're liable to end up in jail." Reaching back, she smoothed Rhona's long, blond hair.

Rhona flinched.

"Don't worry, baby girl. I won't let anything happen to you."

Morris stopped on a narrow dirt road and walked around to the passenger door. He lifted Tessie out and set her down on the shallow bank bordering the roadside. Tall grass scratched her legs.

The sun was going down behind a stand of trees. Dark shadows stretched across the road and a flock of blackbirds flew overhead making strange noises.

A car motor sounded in the distance. Morris glanced at his watch. "That should be him. You stand right there. Don't move."

He ran for the car and drove away. Tessie's mouth opened, but no sound came out. She sniffled, looking in one direction then the other, staring at the barren countryside.

A car drove up and stopped.

She turned to run, but a voice called her name. A voice she knew.

CHAPTER ONE

Tess Howard left the lights of Cedar City, Missouri, behind as she drove out of town, headed for Coffman Park, a strip of woods and hiking trails that would be abandoned at this hour of the night. The urge to turn around and run back home was almost overwhelming. Back to her placid, boring life. Back to safety, if there was such a thing. She was a fool, driving out here alone to meet a stranger, but the load of guilt and grief she carried made it impossible for her to refuse.

At twenty minutes to nine, it was dark enough to use her headlights. The moon wasn't up yet, although stars dotted the sky. She gripped the steering wheel with both hands, concentrating on the area illuminated by her car lights. It had been years since she'd been out this way, and she'd forgotten how isolated it was. Back when she was a teenager, the park had been the site of rowdy parties, not that she'd been allowed to attend, but one of her best friends had died out here, the victim of a drug overdose. These days, it was a favorite spot for hikers and horseback riders, and the occasional marijuana grower.

Trees bordered the narrow strip of barren, empty blacktop stretching in front of her. She flicked her attention left, then right, and then fastened her gaze on the road in front, ignoring the prickling in the back of her neck. She should have told someone where she was going and why. At least they would have some idea where to look if she didn't come back—which was definitely a possibility. Lurid headlines from newspapers and television news programs flashed through her mind. Resolutely, she forced her attention back to the road.

A flash of movement on her left! Tess stomped the brakes as a rabbit scampered across in front of her. She clenched her teeth, biting back a scream.

Her nerves were shot. She was too conscious of the night, too aware of being alone. Everything about this venture was a bad mistake. But she'd come this far. For Rhona's sake, she'd carry it through.

Rhona. Her sister, missing for all these years, but never forgotten. Tess had been four years old and Rhona six when they had been snatched from their beds while their parents were at a charity fundraiser. People thought Tess had been too young to remember what happened. She couldn't forget. The scenes played themselves over and over in her mind, forcing out everything else. The cold, shabby room, the lumpy mattress, the couple who had taken them and held them captive. Morris and Aggie. She had feared them and hated them. And then came the horrible day when Morris had carried her to the car, kicking and screaming, leaving Rhona behind.

She'd never seen her sister again. Her parents had paid the ransom for both of them, but only one child went home. Now this man she was supposed to meet offered information for a price. Would it be Morris, older and meaner? She shoved the thought away. Whatever waited for her, she had to meet this man and hear what he had to say. There would be no rest for her, no healing of the wound she carried in her heart until she knew the truth.

The narrow cleared area of the park came into view, and Tess stopped with the front of her car pointed toward the road in case she needed to leave in a hurry. She shut off the lights. Darkness closed around her. Nothing moved. She sat, shoulders tight and muscles tensed, straining to hear the slightest sound. A beam of light danced through the brush, growing closer. A dark shape walked behind it.

She slowly got out of the car and waited.

The man carrying the light shone it on Tess, illuminating her in its glow but keeping him in shadow. "Did you bring the money?"

"First, I need that information."

"After I get the cash." His voice was low-pitched and harsh, biting off every word.

Tess stiffened, praying for strength. She struggled to hold her voice steady, not let him know she was frightened. "It doesn't work that way. You talk. Then, if you actually have something for me, I'll pay. But first I get the information."

He laughed. "Look, lady. You're out here in the woods all by yourself. If I decide to take that money, you won't have a chance."

Tess forced herself to stay calm. She wanted that information. She needed it. "I agreed to meet you here, but you have to hold up your part of the bargain. Tell me what you know about my sister."

"You'll get your information. Just as soon as I get my hands on that dough. Now hand it over."

Tess felt behind her for the door handle. If she could just get in the car, she'd be safer.

The man lunged toward her. "You're not going anywhere until I get that money."

She raised her hands in a futile gesture to push him away.

There was a sudden rush of movement, a clattering of rocks, and a body hurtled toward them, blasting out of the darkness. Tess toppled backward, crashing into the car then sliding down to hit the ground, knocking the wind out of her. She was dimly aware of the man who had threatened her lying a few feet away.

An explosion of gunfire beat against her eardrums. The man who had barreled into her leaped to his feet and jerked open the back door of her car, lifting and shoving her inside.

Before she could pull herself upright, he slammed the door and dove into the driver's seat, fumbling with the keys. The motor roared to life. The tires slid in the loose gravel, fishtailing a couple of times before gaining traction. The car surged down the road. Another shot exploded.

"You all right?" the driver of the car shouted.

"I think so," she gasped, twisting around to see if they were being followed. Why shoot at her, and who was this guy who had hijacked her car, tossing her around like a rag doll?

She leaned forward, grabbing the edge of the seat. "What happened back there?"

"I'll tell you about it as soon as we get to safety. Where do you live?"

As if she was going to tell him that. But then again, what choice did she have? He had her, he had her car, and someone back there had been shooting at them.

She glanced at her watch. A quarter to ten. Cedar City was a small rural town. They rolled up the sidewalks at night. Nothing would be open except the Git and Go convenience store with a large parking lot that would be practically empty by now.

She gave it some serious thought, and then decided she might as well let him take her home. If he did anything out of line, she could scream loud enough to alert her closest neighbor. Old Mr. Hill would probably blast out of his door, carrying his double-barreled shotgun. She'd be as safe there as anywhere.

Tess took a deep breath, hoping she wasn't about to mess up. "Cedar City."

Thirty minutes later, they reached town, and she gave directions to her house. The car rolled past the wrought-iron fencing circling her yard, entered the gates, and stopped in the driveway.

The driver opened the door for her, and Tess crawled out, feeling bruised and battered. He stood next to her, and she knew she should be afraid, but she'd been shot at, knocked down, and tossed into the back seat like a sack of potatoes. Maybe it was just a delayed reaction to what had happened at the park, but she was royally ticked. She was gearing up to give him a piece of her mind when he grabbed her elbow and turned her around to face the house.

"What are you doing?" she demanded.

"Walking you to the door."

Tess jerked her arm away. "I don't need you to walk me anywhere. Thanks to you, I didn't have a chance to get any information from that man, and now he probably won't contact me again."

"They."

She blinked at him, bewildered. "What did you say?"

"They. There were two of them. One was sneaking up behind you. That's when I got involved. They were also armed, and judging from the way they were throwing lead around, I think there's a very good chance they were planning to kill you. You have any idea why?"

"No, of course not."

Judging from the look he gave her, he didn't believe a word she said. He was right, of course, but she wasn't in a mood to share that information with him.

"Have it your way, but I'm still walking you to the door."

She marched ahead, hearing him trailing along behind, and though she wouldn't admit it, she felt safer having him there, watching her back.

A white two-story Victorian with a wide front porch and a big yard, the house stood a good way back from the street. A large oak tree threw dark shadows over the front steps and entrance. She should have left the porch light on. Would have, if she'd been thinking straight. She unlocked the door and turned on the lights before twisting around to thank him.

He ignored her outstretched hand. "I'm coming in."

Coming in? He could forget that. No way was she inviting him inside. She'd been pushed around enough for one night. It was time to thank this guy and get rid of him. She glared up at him. "I'm not in the habit of allowing strangers into my home. I appreciate what you did for me tonight, but you are not coming into my house."

He gently took her by the shoulders and moved her aside. "Someone was shooting at you back there, and I'm not leaving until I make sure you're all right. You can call the police if you want to. They know me, and they'll vouch for me."

She looked at him. Really looked. Tall and tanned. His dark hair was cut short, and curled crisply on his forehead. A smudge of dirt streaked one high cheekbone, probably from where he had crashed into her attacker. His warm brown eyes gazing into hers were filled with genuine concern. He gave her a heart-stopping smile. There was something familiar about him, as if she had seen him before, but she couldn't remember where.

Although he had released her and stepped back, the warmth from his hands still lingered on her shoulders. He stood watching her, determined and obviously not going anywhere.

She had questions about what had happened at the park, and she wanted answers. Plus, she needed to know who he was and where he had come from. Showing up at just the right time like that was a little too pat. She'd made one bad mistake tonight. Hopefully, this wouldn't be another.

"First, tell me who you are."

"I'm Neil Vaughn, private investigator, and you're Tess Howard. I saw you at the Gibsons', but we weren't introduced."

Now that he mentioned it, she did remember him. She also remembered how practically every woman in the room had vied for his attention, but he hadn't seemed interested in any certain one. At least he was someone she knew, if only casually. She relaxed, feeling a bit safer for the moment.

"What were you doing out there?" she asked.

"It's a long story. Let's sit down, and I'll tell you about it."

Tess led the way into the living room, and watched as he settled into the brown leather recliner that had been her father's favorite chair. She walked to the window to open the curtains. A quick peek assured her that no one was out there, and she pulled them closed again. He hadn't leaned back in the chair, hadn't put out the footstool. His dark eyes studied her, studied the room.

He waited until she was seated before starting. "I've been working on a missing person case. I got an anonymous phone call that someone who had information for me would be waiting at the park tonight. She was supposed to be right where you pulled in and stopped. I saw the first man approach you, heard what you said, and then I saw the second man creeping up behind you. I didn't know what was going on, but since you were outnumbered, I decided it was time for me to lend a hand."

"I see. You were supposed to get information from someone?"

"That's right."

"That's strange. So was I. Don't you think that's a little too much of a coincidence?" She didn't bother to hide her skepticism.

"Could be, but why? And more important, why were you there?"

Instead of answering, she got up and opened a drawer in the oak sideboard, took out a slip of paper and handed it to him. Then she placed a framed picture of a young girl on the coffee table where he could see it, and added a small gold ring with a blue stone, before sitting down and waiting while he read the note aloud. The message was short and simple: "If you want to know where your sister is, bring five thousand dollars to the entrance of Coffman Park, south of town, tonight, eight o'clock. Don't call the police."

He looked up at her. "What's this about? What sister?"

"Twenty-four years ago, my sister and I were kidnapped. Our parents paid the ransom. I was returned, but she wasn't. Ever since then, we've searched for her, but we never found out anything."

"And you think this might be a real contact?"

"I'm hoping it is, but I'm realistic enough to know it might not be. However, that ring came with the note and, as you can see, it's exactly like the one she's wearing in the picture, which makes it seem authentic."

He placed the note on the coffee table, next to the picture and the ring. "I wish I could give you something positive, but my first reaction is to tell the police."

"I can't do that. It would scare him off, and he might be afraid to get in touch with me again." She knew there was a risk—tonight had shown her that—but she couldn't let anything derail her search for Rhona.

"You think he was involved in the kidnapping?"

"I don't know. There were two people I remember, a man and a woman. I still have nightmares about them. But whoever this is, I want to make sure I get the information before I hand over the money. I've been taken in a couple of times, and I don't want that to happen again."

"Aren't you forgetting he was trying to kill you? Why would you want to hear from him?"

Tess twisted her hands in her lap, willing her nerves to settle down. "Because my sister is still missing. Because I'd move heaven and earth to get her back. You don't know what it's been like. Not knowing if she's still alive, not knowing if she's all right or being mistreated. I need to know the truth. I have to know!"

He nodded, looking as if he understood. Of course he couldn't— no one could, not unless they'd lived through it—but at least he wasn't telling her he knew how she felt. She had gotten so tired of hearing that from people who didn't have a clue what it was like to have someone they loved missing.

He picked up the ring, turning it over in his fingers. "I can see why you went out there, but the next time you hear from him—if you do—tell me."

Tess stared at him, trying to understand what he had in mind. Why would he want to get involved in something that could turn violent in an instant? More to the point, what did he have to gain from it? "What could you do?"

"I don't know, but let me do some checking around and see what I can find out. They had a reason for what happened tonight. They were after you. We have to find out why."

He was right, but she wasn't ready to join forces with a stranger. What did she really know about Neil Vaughn? Other than he was easily one of the best-looking men she'd ever seen, which wasn't a good enough reason to trust him.

He stood up, looming over her, so she got up too. She reached out and touched his arm, instantly regretting the impulse. The warmth of his flesh seemed almost too intimate. Tess jerked her hand back, trying to put a little distance between them. "Thank you for what you did tonight, but you don't know me. Why would you want to get mixed up in something like this?"

His gaze caught and held hers, and although she tried to break the connection, she found it impossible to glance away from him. "Look, Tess. The way I see it, you were set up. I can't just turn my back on that and walk away."

She studied him, impressed by the ring of truth in his voice, the determination in his expression. "What if I hire you to find out what this is all about?"

His brown eyes danced with sudden amusement. "Save your money. They took a shot at me, too, so I've got a personal interest in getting to the bottom of this. I'll see you tomorrow, and we're going to sit down and talk about what happened. I'm not joking, Tess. You walked into a trap." He pulled out his cell phone. "Now, I'm going to call a cab and go home. It's getting late, and you need to rest."

"You think they'll come back tonight?" She'd never minded living alone, but tonight the house felt too empty, too silent. Evil had invaded these rooms once before. Could it be lurking again, ready to strike when she least expected it?

"If I did, I wouldn't leave you alone." He took out his wallet, removing a card. "Here's my phone number. If anything disturbs you, call 911 then call me. And don't wait. If you feel something's not right, call. We'll sort it all out later."

She took the card, not saying anything.

He gave her a searching look. "I mean it, Tess. Those men didn't plan to give you any information. They were after something else. Sure, they'd probably have taken the money, but they wanted you dead. Where did you get that note? Did it come in the mail?"

"No, I found it stuck in between the frame and the screen door."

A car horn honked, and he patted her shoulder. "Until tomorrow."

He opened the door and stepped outside, and she felt a strange sense of loss, which was foolish. She was used to being alone. He'd been nice, but she didn't need his help. She didn't need anyone. That wasn't true, and she knew it, but she had to pretend, had to do whatever was required of her, because she'd promised her mother before she died to never give up searching for Rhona. But she didn't have the right to pull someone else into danger with her.

Tess watched him get into the cab. Tall and muscular, he was obviously a man able to take care of himself. She let out a sigh, realizing how long it had been since she had anyone to lean on. Feeling incredibly lonely, she shut the door and faced the empty house. The silence haunted her. She had grown up here without a sister, knowing her parents loved her, but their grief for Rhona had cast a shadow over their lives, stealing the joy from their very existence. She had been a child held in the grip of the memory of being snatched from her home, of losing her sister. Her parents' overwhelming sorrow had damaged her in some way, as if it had been her fault she'd come home and Rhona hadn't.

The glow of the crystal-based table lamp touched the chairs upholstered in muted gold and brown fabric, caressed the bonnet-topped highboy, and glinted off the fret-carved Chippendale mirror. All the comforts she'd enjoyed for the past twenty-four years. What kind of life had Rhona had? And what would she be like now if she were still alive?

Ill at ease, Tess wandered from room to room, making sure that all the downstairs doors were locked. She pulled the curtains closed, shutting out the dark and what it might hold. Then she climbed the stairs to her bedroom, dreading the moment she had to turn out the light. It had been a blessing from God that Neil had shown up when he did, although she still wasn't sure if she believed his story of why he was there. She was slow to take anyone at face value.

But she could have been killed out there. Someone wanted her dead, and she had a feeling she knew why. The will. There couldn't be any other reason. She wasn't a threat to anyone, and the only person who would profit from her death was her missing sister. Was Rhona alive? If so, why wouldn't she try to get in touch? Why send someone else, and why ask for money? Had her sister been behind the threat on her life tonight?

No! She couldn't believe that. Refused to believe it. Rhona had been her big sister, her best friend. Nothing could have changed the way they felt about each other. Tess turned out the light and opened the drapes, staring out at the empty stretch of yard. Tears burned her eyes as she prayed God would help her find her sister.

That night she had trouble sleeping, straining to hear every little sound, imagining someone was creeping through the house. Finally she dozed off, only to dream of that drab room with the lumpy bed where she and Rhona had been held. She heard her sister's voice clearly: "Don't cry, Tessie. Mamma and Daddy will find us. They'll take us home."

She woke with tears on her cheeks.

CHAPTER TWO

Neil called Tess the next morning. She sounded a little grumpy. Probably hadn't slept too well. Neither had he. There was something about being shot at that tended to keep one awake. He needed a ride out to the park, but he wanted to talk to her too, and he planned to accomplish both goals at the same time.

"Hey, how you doing this morning?"

"As well as can be expected, I guess. Why?"

"I need a favor. Would you mind running me out to Coffman Park to pick up my car?" He waited, knowing it was crazy how much he wanted her to say yes.

"I guess so. What time?"

He could hear the grudging tone of her voice and knew exactly how she felt. He was part of something she wanted to forget, pretend it never happened. But it did happen, and it could happen again. He had a hunch the men who had attacked her weren't the kind to give up. She didn't know him very well, either, so she was bound to be a little wary. He couldn't blame her for that. She'd been a victim once. That had to weigh in on how she saw things now.

"Look, Tess. I can get someone else if you prefer, but I thought we might look around out there and see if we can pick up any information on who these guys are. We can't just sit around and wait for them to hit again."

She was silent for a minute, and he could almost hear her hoping he was wrong. "You really think they'll come back?"

Denial was dangerous in a situation like this. "Of course they'll come back. Look, they targeted you. They talked you into coming out there. You got away with the money. Whatever they had in mind, they didn't get it done."

"You're really filling my morning with sunshine, you know that?"

"I'm sorry, but you have to face facts. The more we can find out about them, the better. Now, how about it? Will you drive me out to the park? I need to get my car."

There was a long pause. "All right. Give me twenty minutes."

"That'll be just fine. It'll give me time for a cup of coffee before we start out." He gave her directions to his office, hung up the phone, and leaned back in his chair, thinking of Tess Howard and what had happened last night. Sure, he'd noticed her at the few social functions he'd attended. With hair like spun gold and eyes as blue as a summer sky, she'd been hard to miss, but something about her intrigued him.

Maybe it was the haunted look in those blue eyes, or the way she could be in the middle of a public gathering—everyone laughing and talking—and suddenly seem as if she were only present in body. As if the spirit, the essence of her, had been whisked away to some place no one could follow.

Her parents had created a foundation for the recovery of missing children. Child Search, or something like that. From what he'd heard, they'd had some success in recovering several children, but apparently they hadn't learned anything about the one that mattered most to them. Rhona Howard was still missing. Which brought up the question: Why, after twenty-four years, was someone offering to sell information about her? Why now?

• • •

Tess hung up the receiver and sat for a minute staring out the window. Why would Neil Vaughn want her to go out to the park with him? He was a trained investigator. Why would he need her to help him look? His claim that he was there to get information was flimsy at the least. What were the odds that both of them would receive the same message from two different people to meet at the park at the same time, same place, to get information about two entirely different things?

Look at it that way, and she had ample reason not to trust Neil Vaughn. Her family had money and a successful business, and it had led some people to attempt to take advantage of them by trying to sell fraudulent information about Rhona. Tess had learned not to trust anyone until they had proven themselves.

No matter how she felt, the man needed his car.

She dressed then drove to meet Neil. The office was located in a one-story white bungalow that used to be a family dwelling. Black and gold lettering on the window read Neil Vaughn, Private Investigator. She sat looking at it, then reluctantly got out and climbed the steps.

• • •

The office door opened and Tess stepped inside. Today she wore jeans and a white T-shirt covered with a short-sleeved blue shirt the exact color of her eyes. Her golden hair fell to her shoulders, framing her face. Neil smiled appreciatively. This was one beautiful woman.

She stood by the door, waiting. "If you're ready, let's go."

"I'm ready." He got to his feet and followed her, stopping to lock the door. She walked ahead of him, giving him a good view of the graceful way she moved, the way her hair glinted in the morning sunlight.

Once they were on the road, she glanced over at him. "I'm not thrilled about going back to the place where someone took a shot at me."

"I understand that, but we need to check it out just in case they left anything behind."

She stopped at the intersection and shot him a questioning look. "Where were you? You blasted out of nowhere and took us both down. Why were you that close to where we were talking? It seems awfully convenient for you to show up like that."

She didn't completely trust him. Neil was surprised at how much that bothered him. He'd have to go slow. Judging from what he'd seen of her, Tess Howard didn't allow closeness, which was fine with him. He wasn't in a position to encourage closeness either. He needed to keep this just a working relationship. Strictly business.

"I told you. I got a phone call from a woman about a case I'm working on. She insisted I meet her out there last night, and she'd tell me what I needed to know. It sounded like a scam, but I figured I could take care of myself. What I didn't count on was a couple of guys with guns."

"You were supposed to meet her at the same spot?" She pulled out to pass a slow-moving pickup. "Do you know how contrived that sounds?"

"I know exactly how it sounds, but it's the truth. I didn't trust her all that much, so I parked at one of the trailheads and walked back. I was hiding behind a tree when this car pulled in and you got out. Then I saw the light bobbing around out in the brush. So I sat tight, waiting to see what was coming down."

"And you think maybe we were both set up?"

"It looks that way, but we don't know anything for sure yet."

They approached the park entrance, and Tess braked. "What now?"

"Just keep going to the first trailhead on the right. I pulled my car off the road and parked behind a stand of sumac. Didn't want to leave it out where it could be seen."

Her expression was still skeptical. "I'm not familiar with this area. You'll have to tell me where to go."

"It's the next entrance. There's a clear spot for parking."

She stepped on the gas, driving past the main entrance. "Go on. You were telling me what you saw. What happened next?"

He shifted to face her. "Like I said, I saw the guy come up close to you, and I could hear what you were talking about. Then I saw a second guy sneaking up behind you, and I figured since you were outnumbered I'd better lend a hand. You know the rest."

She took her gaze off the road long enough to glance at him. "So, really, why do you think you were there? Do you seriously believe someone had information for you, or were you supposed to be shot too? Is that it?"

Neil considered the question. He couldn't think of anyone who would hate him enough to kill him, unless some of the people he'd help bring to justice in New York had followed him here—which didn't seem possible, and wouldn't have anything to do with Tess.

"I don't know why they wanted me there, but we're going to pick up my car and drive back to the park entrance and look it over. Maybe we'll find something that will shed some light on what's going on."

Tess pulled in where he indicated and stopped in front of the thicket of sumac bushes. Neil sat still, making no effort to get out. It was natural she'd have questions. After all, they were practically strangers, but he was serious about learning the identity of the men who had attacked them last night. Lips pressed tight and wearing a stubborn scowl, she stared out the windshield. Finally she turned to face him. "This is my fight. It doesn't concern you, and I don't want you involved."

"Someone lures me out here, and I don't know who or why. I get shot at, and there's a good chance someone might show up to finish the job, and you don't want me involved? What are you thinking?"

She flushed, turning her cheeks rose-petal pink, which made her even more beautiful. He brushed the thought aside. He wasn't angling to start a relationship with her. He was just trying to keep her safe.

"I didn't intend to upset you," she said. "It's just that I don't want anyone hurt trying to help me."

"I don't want either of us to get hurt, but you might as well understand I'm in this until the end, whether you want me there or not. Now, you drive back to the park entrance, and I'll follow."

He opened the door and got out, not bothering to see if she was angry or not. He didn't care how she felt. Did she honestly think he could turn his back and pretend last night never happened? Was that what she thought of him? And why did he care so much about her opinion?

Neil got in his car and followed Tess back to the entrance. They parked, and he got out and pointed to tire tracks dug into the gravel. "I did that taking off last night. Now, let's spread out and start looking. If you find anything, yell."

Tess wandered off, but Neil stood in one spot, looking intently at the scuffed dirt where he had knocked her to the ground. It had to have shaken her. Probably bruised her a little. He realized how brave she'd been, coming out here all by herself. She was serious about finding her sister. That was enough to prove to him that she was on the level. She came out here expecting to learn some information. He came out here for the same reason. And neither of them got what they wanted. But neither did the guys who were waiting for them. Which pretty well guaranteed they'd be back. He had to learn something fast, before anything else happened.

Tess approached and Neil waited, attention centered on the slip of paper she held.

"What's that?"

"A receipt from Motel 6. You think they could have been staying there?"

She held it out to him, and he took the receipt, looking it over. "Worth checking out. We're not finding anything else here, so let's go. You lead the way, I'll follow."

On the ten-minute drive to the motel, Neil thought about Tess and her story of being kidnapped. He'd spent time on the Internet last night, looking for references to the crime, finding a ton of them, all saying pretty much the same thing: two little girls, Rhona, six, and Tess, four, had been taken from their home. A teenage girl who had been babysitting while the parents were at a fundraising dinner party had been knocked in the head, tied up, and left behind. The girl claimed to have seen nothing.

Thank goodness for the Internet. A little know-how and plenty of time could usually turn up information about almost anything. After a couple of hours on the computer searching through old TV news archives, he'd finally found a digitized copy of old film footage, showing Tess's parents begging for the return of Rhona, their faces strained with worry, voices shaking. Why take both girls then just return one? And what had happened to the one who hadn't come back?

To this day, no one had seen or heard from Rhona Howard. So where did these guys last night come from, and why? Did they actually know something about the missing sister?

The woman behind the desk at Motel 6 was plump, medium height, with white hair cut short on the sides and erupting into a halo of curls on top. She leaned her arms on the desk. "May I help you?"

Neil placed the receipt on the counter and smiled. "Can you tell us something about this?"

She pushed up her glasses with one finger and stared at him for a minute. "Who's asking?"

He fished his private investigator's credentials out of his wallet and handed it to her. "I'm looking for information about an attempted assault last night. This receipt was found in the vicinity. The person who dropped it probably didn't have anything to do with the attack, but I have to eliminate anyone who might not have been involved."

"I see." She turned to the register, running her finger down the page. "It shows here that a Morris Clark rented the room and paid in advance with cash. I don't know when he checked out. The keys were left in the room, and he apparently didn't stop by the office."

Tess gasped softly. Neil resisted the urge to look at her, wanting to downplay his questions, but he had an idea what was wrong. Morris Clark was the name of the man who had kidnapped her. Was he back? And if so, why?

"Can you describe him?" He tried to keep the urgency out of his voice, but the woman behind the counter gave him an alert glance. He'd have to be more careful.

She looked thoughtful. "Let's see. Medium height, around five seven or eight, I guess. A little hefty, sandy hair, thinning on top, hazel eyes, features a little flabby, crooked front teeth with one lapping over the other a little, and his breath smelled like mint. I guess that's all. Of course, I just got a glimpse at him."

Just a glimpse? If she ever got tired of working in the motel office, he might hire her. She had seen more in just that one glimpse than most people would notice in a week. He thanked the woman— her name was Andrea Grimes—and they left.

Outside, Tess climbed into her car and slammed the door. He approached and she rolled the window down, her voice curt. "If you don't need me anymore, I'm going back to town."

"No, that's okay. Thanks for helping me out." He watched as she drove out of the motel parking lot. He'd give her time to calm down and then try to talk to her. If he was going to keep her safe and find out who had attacked her, he would need her help.

Back at the office, Neil sat down to read over his notes and the printed Internet files. After an hour he shoved the papers aside and rubbed his eyes. He knew a lot more now about the Howard girls and their kidnapping, but so far he hadn't found any reason to involve him. He had a hunch that the call sending him out to the park was because someone wanted him out there when Tess showed up. Was his dead body supposed to be found with hers? If so, why? He'd never heard of Rhona Howard before last night, and he only had a passing acquaintance with Tess, although he had a feeling that they were going to get to know each other much better before this was over, and that could create a problem.

After the woman he'd planned to marry had been killed, he'd steered clear of women, feeling he didn't have a right to get involved with anyone else. He'd put Rebecca in a dangerous position, promised to keep her safe, protect her from the people who wanted her dead, and he'd failed. Her death had almost destroyed him. He couldn't go through that again. He'd do whatever it took to keep Tess safe, but for both of their sakes, he had to keep everything between them on a business level.

The phone rang, and he reached for it. "Hello?"

"Neil? This is Tess Howard."

"Yeah, Tess. How you doing?"

"I'm doing all right, but I have something I want to talk to you about. Could you come out to the house for a little while?"

"Sure. What time?"

"Well, what about now? Or is that too soon for such short notice?"

"No. I'm not doing anything important. I'll be there in a few minutes."

• • •

Tess answered Neil's knock on the door, holding it open to let him step inside. She looked up at him, hoping the carefully applied makeup would hide all evidence of the tears she'd shed. The way her heart leaped when she saw him caught her by surprise. After all, he was practically a stranger. There was too much at stake to get careless just because Neil Vaughn was standing there smiling down at her.

"I'm sorry I left so abruptly. It was nice of you to just drop every- thing and come."

"No problem. Is there anything I can help you with?"

"I want to show you something."

She led the way into the living room. When he was settled in the brown leather recliner, she picked up a sheaf of papers from the coffee table. "You asked last night why anyone would want to kill me. I think I know."

He cocked an eyebrow at her. "Oh yeah? Someone you've made mad enough to try to wipe you out? Like who?"

"No, nothing like that. My parents never got over losing Rhona. Oh, they loved me and were glad to have me back, but an important part of our family was missing. You don't just get over something that horrible."

"No, I guess not. So where are you going with this?"

"Before she died, my mother made a new will. We'd had some people calling us about Rhona, claiming that she was alive, people wanting money to tell what they knew, stuff like that."

"Did you pay any of them?"

"A couple, but we never got anything in exchange. Nothing helpful, anyway. They were just scams. None of the leads panned out, but Mom never gave up hope. She couldn't. Giving up would mean that she didn't think Rhona would ever be found."

"So she made out a will?"

"Yes. She left all of her property to be divided equally between her two daughters, me and Rhona. Her attorney, Herbert Davis, objected to her plans, pointing out she was leaving a legal mess for me if an imposter ever showed up claiming to be Rhona. But it was what she wanted, and he couldn't talk her out of it."

"What if Rhona never comes back?"

"As long as I'm alive, I'm trustee for her share. Her profits are to be kept in a separate account, drawing interest. If I never find her, then on my death her part goes to Child Search, the foundation my parents established. My share is mine to do with as I see fit for as long as I live. I can, of course, leave it to my husband and children, if I have any, but if I never marry and Rhona outlives me and comes home, then my share will go to her in payment for all the years she wasn't with us. If she never comes back and I stay single, then mine will go to the foundation, too."

"You think they were trying to kill you so she could inherit your part as well as hers?"

"It's a possibility." Actually, she felt it was more than that. Hearing Morris Clark's name had brought back all the horror of their captivity. Would he kill for profit? Of course. After all, he had kidnapped a couple of children and held them for ransom.

"So you're saying your mother might have, in effect, signed your death warrant."

"That's not the point. Don't you see? If someone is trying to inherit the money, she's still alive."

• • •

Neil hated to dampen her enthusiasm, but he had to point out the obvious. Just saying something didn't make it true. She needed more evidence. "Not necessarily. This could be a scam."

"But the will—"

"How could the men last night have known anything about the will? I don't think that's why they met you in an isolated area and then tried to ambush you. There must be something else."

She stared at him, and he could see how much she hated to agree. "Then why would they try to get money out of me? There had to be a reason."

"I did some Internet surfing last night, and brought along the information I found. You want to go over it and see if we can find anything new?"

She nodded, but seemed reluctant. Probably didn't want to give up on her theory of the will. "Bring it into the kitchen, and we can spread it out on the table."

Seated at the round oak table with cups of fresh coffee, they went through the pages, reading intently. Neil had already gone over the information, but he read it again, slowly and carefully, trying to catch anything he might have missed, but nothing jumped out at him. Two girls had been taken, their family devastated. The kidnappers had never been caught.

Tess looked up from the page she held. "I remember the night they took us. We shared a room, and I woke up to see a strange woman bending over me. She pulled me out of the bed and wrapped me in a quilt. The man did the same with Rhona, and then they took us down the stairs and put us in an old car, and drove off. We were crying, and the woman slapped us and yelled for us to shut up."

The woman had slapped two terrified little girls? Just thinking about it made him furious. Gave him another goal besides finding out who had shot at them. He also intended to find the people responsible for kidnapping those two kids. It was outrageous that trash like that could hurt innocent people and get away with it.

They read in silence for a while, and he noticed Tess having to stop occasionally to catch her breath. It was all here. Just dry information someone had written, but he knew for her it came alive on the page. She looked up and caught him watching.

"You okay?" he asked. "Is this too hard for you?"

"This isn't the first time I've read most of this. We have it on file at the foundation office and I've gone over it before, but it's been a long time since I've looked at it. The people who took us just vanished. The police did everything they could, but the kidnappers didn't leave much behind in the way of evidence. But I'd give everything I own to learn what happened to her. My parents poured their lives into finding her. Now I'm the only one left to do the job. If there's any chance at all of finding her, I have to help in any way I can. Failure isn't an option. That would be a betrayal of everyone I ever loved."

He'd expected her to be determined to find her sister. After all, she'd risked her life trying to get information, but this bordered on obsession. Would she be able to cope if they never found Rhona? From the intensity in her voice, he suspected failure would destroy her.

"We'll do everything we can to find the truth. I promise you that. But you need to keep notes. Write down everything you remember, no matter how small. We don't know what little piece of information might hold the key to something big."

"All right. I'll start now." She got up and left the room, returning with a couple of spiral notebooks. "Here, one for you, one for me."

He took the book and opened it to the first page. "I've been jotting notes down as I go. I'll go back and put them in the notebook so I'll have them all together."

A few minutes later, Tess slapped the table. "It says here that the police thought the kidnappers could have been a couple of men who worked for my father, but the names are wrong. The people who had us were named Morris and Aggie Clark. She was skinny and mean. Or she was mean to me. She liked Rhona. I can remember her brushing my sister's hair and calling her Baby Girl. She acted like she hated me."

"Is that the reason you left the motel like that? You think it's the same guy?"

She met his gaze unflinchingly, and he read the truth in her eyes. She might not admit it, but she was sure the kidnapper had found her again.

"I think it's possible. When I heard his name, it hit me how much I hated him and how mean he was. I had to get away."

"You were four years old. How can you remember much about it?"

"Rhona was my big sister. She took care of me. When Aggie hit me, Rhona would hold me and tell me not to cry. And then they separated us, and I've never seen her again."

Tears rolled down her face, unheeded. He wanted to reach over and put his arm around her, comfort her, but she would probably reject him. From what little he knew of her, Tess Howard wasn't used to relying on anyone.

Now she looked at him, eyes sparkling through her tears. "I've been praying about it, and I get this peaceful feeling when I ask God to help me. I'm going to keep on trusting. With His help, I'll find her."

He wanted to ask if her parents had prayed for Rhona to be returned, but something held him back. He was a believer. Or at least he used to be, but he hadn't been to church in years. He'd pretty much given up on God doing anything to help.

Tess drew a deep breath and sat a little straighter. Something in her expression warned him. She was building up to saying something he wasn't going to like.

She tilted her chin and stared at him, as if daring him to disagree with her. "Since I'm convinced this involves the will, it's apparent this is a family problem. It can't concern you, so I'd like for you to back off and let me handle it."

Neil shook his head, making no effort to hide the fact that he thought this was ridiculous. "No, Tess. It's not going to be like that."

"I don't see why not. It's not your problem, and I don't want to take a chance on someone getting hurt. They have something I want, and I'm willing to pay for it. And at the next meeting, I'll pick the time and the place."

"Okay, one, I'm already involved. Whoever sent me out to the park that night pulled me into whatever is going on. Second, there is no way I'm going to walk off and leave you to deal with these characters by yourself. And third, I'm in this to the end, whether you want me or not. In fact, I'm not all that interested in what you want."

He reached into his briefcase and brought out a handful of papers. "I've got to go, but I made copies of everything I found. From what you've said, you probably have most of it on file at the office, but I'll leave this with you anyway. Here's the rest of your copy. I'll take mine with me, and if I learn anything, I'll let you know. You do the same with me."

Her mouth tightened. She wasn't happy with him, but that was her problem. She followed him to the door, although she didn't say anything else. He looked in the rearview mirror as he drove away. She was still standing in the doorway, looking so alone he almost turned around and went back, but he couldn't come up with a believable reason for doing so. He'd do his best to keep her safe, but those men last night hadn't been playing around. That note had been delivered to her home. They knew where she lived.

CHAPTER THREE

Tess spent another restless night. Morris Clark's name showing up unexpectedly had brought back all the memories of that dreadful time when she and her sister had been held captive. She had a strange conviction, though, that Rhona was out there, waiting to be found, as if they were reaching the end of their separation. Her sister was coming home. She didn't know why she felt that way, but the feeling was too strong to be denied.

Maybe it was because Neil was helping her, and she wasn't alone anymore. She wanted to trust him, but she still had questions. He came across as being the kind of man who would do something just because it was right. If he was on the level, then God must have sent him to her, knowing how badly she needed someone. She'd been a little short of people to depend on after her parents died.

Tess was getting ready to go to work when the phone rang. She answered to find Frank Walpin, the attorney who now ran Herbert Davis's law firm. His voice vibrated with tension. "Tess. I need to see you. May I come by the house this morning? This isn't anything I want anyone to overhear me talking about."

"Of course. What time?"

"Say in about thirty minutes. And Tess, I don't want anyone else there. Just the two of us. This is important."

"All right, Frank. I'll be here." She hung up the receiver and slumped in her chair. What now? After Herbert died and Frank had taken over as her attorney, it had been one thing after another. Just little things, something that could have been solved with a bit of common sense, but Frank had insisted she get involved. She had a hunch he was trying to leave his mark on her business, maybe even on the foundation her parents had established, making her depend on him.

What he didn't know was that her father had trained her to take his place, making her start in at the bottom of Howard Manufacturing, and work her way to the top. She knew every job in the company, had worked most of them, and took great pride in the top-of-the-line designer furniture they created. Her employees liked her and were loyal. Her business was stable and doing well. She ran the foundation, too, and she didn't need his help.

When Frank arrived, she opened the door and ushered him into the living room. He sat down on the couch and looked around. "You haven't changed anything since your mother's death."

"No. I like it the way it is."

He smiled, handsome, but way too sure of himself to suit her. Tall, fit, with dark hair and a narrow black mustache, he could have played the part of a movie hero in any number of romantic films.

He made her nervous.

Frank always seemed to stand too close, smile too broadly, as if something special existed just between the two of them. But he had a wife, and Tess wasn't into fooling around with a married man, if that was what he had in mind.

Now he leaned forward, as if imparting a great secret. "I have something to tell you. It's not definite yet, but I feel sure enough to bring it to your attention."

She stared at him, bewildered. Was this big secret something personal for him? Something concerning Gloria, his wife—the woman she had never been able to figure out? One minute Gloria was sweet and concerned, the next cold and aloof—not someone who made friends easily. But then, with a husband like Frank, maybe she had to be on guard with other females.

He smiled. "You won't believe it when I tell you, but I've found a young woman—or rather, she found me—who just might be Rhona."

Stunned into silence, Tess stared at him. Goosebumps broke out on her arms. "What?"

"I'm running a background check trying to learn more about her. Now, mind you, I'm not sure, but there's a strong possibility it's her. I'm researching her information, doing a little digging. So far, I haven't turned up any real proof, but it's interesting. Keep your fingers crossed."

"After all this time? I can't believe it. Where has she been? Is she using Rhona's name?"

"I can't divulge any information yet, and besides, I want to make sure she's who she claims to be, before getting you involved. We don't want to make any mistakes. This is too important to mess up."

"Surely you can tell me what name she's using? Let the foundation check it out for you. We have methods of finding people. Give us her name, and we'll run a check for social security numbers, addresses, people who know her. We can do a lot to help you."

This was what she had prayed about for all these years, and just this morning she had felt God would answer those prayers. Why, then, didn't she feel any sense of elation? Was it because she had hoped before only to have those hopes dashed? No matter how much she wanted it to be true, a part of her mind was warning her not to go too fast, to be cautious. She'd been taken advantage of too many times to trust easily.

"When can I meet her?" Surely, if she saw this woman face to face, there would be something familiar, something to show her the truth.

"Not yet. Don't go too fast here. We need to be sure. Like I said, I'm having her checked out, but I wanted to warn you in case she decides to bypass me and go directly to you. I'll use the foundation after I learn a little more about her. We can't afford to be fooled on this. There's too much at stake."

Too much at stake? Yes, the business, the house. Enough to entice an impostor, but none of it meant as much to her as getting her sister back. "All right, but don't keep me waiting too long. I want to see this woman. I need to talk to her. I could ask her questions no one else would know to ask."

"Why don't you make me a list of those questions? I could ask her then check her answers."

Tess instinctively rejected his request. This wasn't something she could leave to someone else. She needed to pray about it, ask God to help her make the right decision. "No. I want to question her myself. I need to see her expression, watch how she talks. Hear the tone of her voice. This is something I have to do. I assume you will use DNA to make sure, right?"

His expression changed subtly. She had offended him. He ended the conversation by standing as if preparing to leave. "If that's what you want, of course. When I'm fairly sure we have the right woman, I'll bring her to you. Let's leave it at that for now, and if anyone tries to get in touch with you, refer them to my office. Just trust me, Tess. I'll make sure no one takes advantage of you."

She watched as he left, closing the door behind him, then she fell to her knees beside the couch, letting the tears fall. "Oh, God, please, please let it be Rhona. I've waited for so long. Help me, Lord. Give me wisdom to know the right thing to do. I can't bear to be fooled by someone just pretending to be her, but I couldn't live with myself if I thought I'd driven her away by not believing what she says."

She stayed on her knees for a long time, before pulling herself up to sit on the couch. She had to do something, talk to someone, but Frank had cautioned her to be careful. Tess got to her feet. She would discuss it with Neil. It went against her better judgment to get involved with him too much, but she believed he would listen and give her good advice. She called the plant, telling the receptionist that she would be late, and then drove to Neil's office.

Something else bothered her. Why would Frank want to keep it such a secret, and why wouldn't he want her to meet this woman? She wasn't sure she could completely trust Frank Walpin. After all, if his wife couldn't trust him, who could?

Neil greeted her with a smile. "Hey, come in. What's going on?"

Tess sat down across the desk from him and took a deep breath. "I know I said I don't want you involved, and I still don't. But I have to talk to someone. Frank Walpin came to see me."

"The attorney? What did he want?"

"He said he's found a woman who claims to be Rhona, and he thinks there's a possibility she really might be."

He didn't say anything, just looked at her.

"Neil?"

"Yeah. I'm still trying to take in what you're saying."

"I know. It stunned me too. "

"Tess, go slow on this. She could turn out to be an impostor, and it would tear you apart if you put your faith in her."

Tess nodded, knowing he had immediately understood what she couldn't bring herself to admit. She'd been disappointed before. How could she trust now?

She took a deep breath and exhaled. "Frank told me not to tell anyone until he checked her out, but I had to talk to someone who would understand. You're a private investigator so you know more about something like this than I do. I need help and I don't know where else to turn."

"I'm glad you came to me and I promise I'll do everything I can to help you. Look, let it rest for a few days. I mean, you get a note about information concerning your missing sister, and almost immediately a woman claiming to be her shows up. All of this after nothing for twenty-four years? I'll get Bob Gorman to help me, and we'll do some digging. There has to be something out there, and we'll find it."

She realized he was right, but she still felt deflated, knowing this wasn't what she had hoped he would say. "I guess I wanted you to tell me it had to be her. I'll calm down, if you'll let me know if you find out anything."

"The very minute I learn something," he promised. "We're working on this together, and we'll be a hard team to beat."

"I hope so, but, it shouldn't be so easy for someone to just drop out of sight and never be seen again."

"It happens every day, but so does the opposite—people finding family they never even knew they had. Keep praying, Tess. That's the best thing we've got going for us."

"I will. Have you found anything at all?"

"Maybe. Come around to the computer and take a look."

Tess walked behind the desk to look over his shoulder, close enough to catch the scent of his aftershave, something spicy and masculine. She was intensely aware of the way his dark green T-shirt accentuated the muscular curve of his shoulders. A new file flashed across the screen, and the words caught her attention. She grabbed the back of Neil's chair. According to the website, Morris Clark was in prison—Jefferson City Correctional Center, to be exact. Had been for the past five years. He wouldn't be up for parole for another year. So why was the man who rented the room at Motel 6 using Morris Clark's identification?

Neil clicked on a new site bringing up a picture of Clark. The real Morris was a big guy, looked like a linebacker, with a thick head of gray hair. The big smile he gave the camera showed perfect teeth. She recognized him instantly. Older, but still the same.

"This guy doesn't match the description Andrea gave us at the motel. I'd say we can be sure that wasn't Morris Clark shooting at us. Do you recognize him? Is he the one who took you and your sister?"

"That's him. He's older, but I remember him."

Tess realized she had backed up a step, feeling an irrational surge of fear. He was in prison. He couldn't hurt her now. But she'd seen that face in her worse dreams, seen those lips twisted into a sneer, heard that cruel jeering laugh when he'd carried her away from Rhona. She'd lived with it for too many years to ever forget.

"I wish I'd had a good look at the men who shot at us. Do you have any idea how to look for them?"

Neil shook his head. "I have the phone call from the woman wanting me to be out at the park. Luckily, it recorded, but I don't recognize her voice. She sounded like an older woman, and here's another problem. How could she have learned about the case I'm working on? I'll go back over every note, every conversation I have in that file, looking for a connection. "

"You have a recording of the phone call? I'd like to hear it." It might help answer some of the questions she had about him.

He looked at her for a moment, and she had a feeling he knew exactly what she was thinking by asking him to play it. Finally he shrugged and leaned over to turn it on.

A woman's voice filled the silence. "Mr. Vaughn. I hear you're looking for information about Ralph Wheeler. If you'll come to the Coffman Park entrance tonight at eight o'clock, I'll have the information you need."

The call ended, leaving Tess frowning in concentration. That voice! It sounded vaguely familiar. Had she really heard it before, or was she jumping at shadows? She looked at Neil and found him watching her.

"Satisfied now that I really did get a phone call?" he asked

"Yes, I suppose so, but you have to admit it sounded strange when we were both there for the same reason."

"Maybe so, but that's exactly what happened. Now we have to find out who sent those messages, and why."

"All right. I'll help. Just tell me what to do."

Their eyes met, and her heart skipped a beat. Why did she let him affect her this way? She needed to get her emotions under control before she lost sight of the main goal: finding her sister.

"We might see if we can find information on any of Morris Clark's buddies. Somehow this guy got his identification. What was the name of the woman who helped kidnap you?" Neil asked.

"Aggie. I assume they were married, but maybe not. I really don't know. At least it's something to look for."

"I'll see what I can discover about Aggie Clark. Maybe there's a police record that would tell us something."

It was like she had a clock ticking in her mind, and time was moving much too fast. "Keep what I told you about Frank a secret for a while, will you? I don't want to do anything to scare the mystery woman away. Maybe she really is Rhona. If she's not, we might learn something from her that will help us find the real one."

Neil nodded. "Right. But we're going to do all we can to find out the truth. Stay in touch if you find anything I need to know."

Suddenly she was too aware of his presence, too conscious of the deep timbre of his voice. She moved away, putting the desk between them. "I will. You too."

She opened the door and left, feeling she was walking out of a safe haven into a hostile world, which wasn't very realistic. This was Cedar City, her town.

She realized she hadn't eaten since breakfast. It might be a good idea to stop in at Country Kitchen for lunch. She didn't feel like cooking. Besides, she needed a good meal, not just scrounging what she could find in the refrigerator. The restaurant, built to look like a log cabin with a shake shingle roof, had several cars in the parking lot. Inside, antique cooking utensils decorated the walls along with paintings of barns in rural settings.

A new waitress was hopping from table to table, taking orders and clearing away dirty dishes. She stopped by Tess's table, smiling at her. "Are you ready to order yet?"

"I'll have the special, and a glass of tea."

"Anything else?"

"No, that will do." Tess watched as she walked away. Maybe a couple of inches taller than she was, dark hair cut in a pixie, blue eyes, and a friendly manner. She liked her on sight. Funny how it was that way with some people. You could see them once and know if you'd like them or not.

When the waitress brought her food, she smiled and introduced herself. "I'm Tess Howard. Are you new in town?"

The woman paused for a moment and looked back over her shoulder, as if not sure she should be visiting with a customer. "Yes. I'm Maxine Crowley. I was passing through and noticed the help wanted sign on the door, and this looked like a nice place, so I decided to give it a try."

"I've lived here all my life. The people are friendly, and it's a good town. I'm sure you'll like it."

"I hope so. It reminds me of a place where I used to live. They say you can't go back, but I wonder if that's right."

"I guess it depends on where you're trying to go back to. I've always thought, if you're going to a place where you had friends and people who loved you, they'd welcome you back."

A strange expression crossed Maxine's face, but then she gave a tentative smile. "Well, time will tell, I suppose. It's been nice talking to you, but I'd better get back to work."

She turned away to clear used dishes off a couple of tables. Tess had never seen Maxine Crowley before in her life, but she reminded her of someone. After thinking about it, she brushed the thought aside. She had too many more important things to think about. Like this woman that Frank thought might be Rhona. She hoped with all her heart it would be her sister, but she needed to take Neil's advice and go slow. She didn't dare jump in too fast and mess this up, but she prayed her search was coming to an end. If only it could have happened while her parents were alive. One thing for sure, she was going to her office at Child Search and look through those files pertaining to her family again. There might be something she had overlooked.

• • •

Tess entered the office of Child Search and stopped to talk to Rose Schneider, the office manager. She didn't have time to oversee every detail of the foundation and run the business, too. Besides, Rose knew more about the process of looking for missing people than Tess could ever learn. When she was growing up, her mother had been in charge of the foundation. Tess had worked with her father in the business. She had seldom been involved with Child Search.

When her parents started this foundation, they had concentrated on finding missing children, but eventually they expanded to looking for anyone who had disappeared. The process was complicated and difficult.

The public didn't realize how many times people disappeared, never to be seen again. Or how many times it could be children—children walking home from school, children in stores or parking lots, or even playing in their own yard. And all too often it was just grab and snatch. Nothing left behind to show what had happened. Sometimes they got lucky. Sometimes the police did, too. Sometimes everyone failed.

Like in this case. They even had a name, Morris and Aggie Clark. But the Clarks had vanished as completely as Rhona Howard did. She finished talking to Rose and located the file she needed. Alone in her office she went through the records again. Most of it was what Neil had brought her to read. Except for the reports from the private investigators. But each report said the same thing. Nothing. They sent a bill of course, but no one had found any trace of Rhona or the Clarks.

People could change their name, change their identification, and change their looks. There were many ways to hide, and from what time she had spent here, she had learned more of them than she wanted to know. Sometimes the foundation got lucky in the search for a child, but had never found Rhona.

Tess blinked back tears, praying it would be different this time. But she couldn't accept anything at face value. Frank had to work with her, whether he wanted to or not.

CHAPTER FOUR

Neil parked in the driveway in front of Tess's house and sat for a minute, dreading to go inside. He was going to ask her to go back in memory to a time that she needed to move past. He'd had his own problems with moving past something, and he'd learned the hard way that some memories can grip the mind so completely they're impossible to forget. Finally he opened the car door and got out, walking toward the front steps. Tess's house was a Victorian home, not as fancy as some, but elegant, like her. She was a beautiful woman, and at one time he'd have wanted to develop a relationship with her, but that was before life left him scarred and unfit. He wasn't sure he could give love again.

He tapped on the door and Tess opened it almost immediately. He had a feeling she'd been standing at the front window, watching him. The thought pleased him until he remembered he was keeping this strictly on a business level.

"Neil. I wasn't expecting you today. Come on in."

He stepped inside, and was immediately struck by the peacefulness of the surroundings. This wasn't a house decorated just for show. It was a home, and it showed the results of living. The mementos scattered around were family things. The paintings on the wall appeared to have been chosen because they were liked, not because they were decorator-approved. He found himself wishing he could afford a house like this. Maybe someday, after he got his business built up the way he wanted it.

"Are we meeting in the living room or the kitchen?" Tess asked.

"How about the kitchen. It will be easier to take notes if we need to."

"The kitchen it is." She led the way, and Neil smiled appreciatively at the graceful way she walked, the easy-fitting jeans, the black top, and the turquoise long-sleeved shirt worn unbuttoned and swinging past her waist. Tess was a woman to catch any man's eye, and she was brave and compassionate along with it. Even though he wasn't looking for companionship, he couldn't help sparing a thought for what might have been if things were only different.

They sat down at the kitchen table, and she looked at him expectantly. "Have you learned anything new?"

"Not really. Have you heard any more about the woman who claims to be Rhona?" Why was it taking so long to arrange a meeting? He'd have thought that would have been one of the first steps.

"No. I left a message for Frank, but he hasn't called back. I'm beginning to lose patience."

The phone rang, and she sprang up to answer. Neil heard her gasp and then cry, "No! No! Rhona!"

He leaped to his feet, covering the distance between them in two steps. She sagged against him as he took the receiver from her and clamped it to his ear. It took him a moment to realize what he was hearing: a young girl crying great, gulping sobs. "Momma. I want my Momma! Tessie? Where are you?"

He was hearing the pitiful cry of a child kidnapped twenty-four years ago and never allowed to return home.

The phone line went dead. He replaced the receiver and closed his arms around Tess. Her tears wet his shirt. Her body was racked with sobs so deep they seemed to tear her apart. He stood embracing her until she took one last gasping, body-shuddering sob and looked up at him.

"That was Rhona."

Either that, or someone very good at pretending. It had sounded real enough that the hairs on his arms prickled at the remembered pain in the young voice.

"I had forgotten."

The words were almost whispered, so soft he had to lean close to hear.

"Forgot what, Tess?"

She took a deep breath and stepped out of his arms, leaving them curiously empty. "We had calls like that after I came home. No one ever said anything, no one ever asked for money. It was like they were just playing those tapes of her over and over to torment us."

"You're sure they were tapes?"

At her startled expression, he hastened to explain. "I know this one was. But the earlier ones were tapes, too, not her actually crying into the phone?"

"There were just a few of them, and after a while we recognized them, the same ones played again and again."

"You said your family received the phone calls after you were returned home. You were just a young child. How could you remember them so well?"

"I remember my mother crying and my dad sitting at the kitchen table, hiding his face in his hands. I watched what it did to them. And we got the calls again after I was old enough to understand what I was hearing. It tore me apart. Made me afraid to answer the phone for a long time. It's like our family was under siege."

"It sounds personal, like the kidnapper knew your family and had a grudge against them. Maybe an employee, or someone who'd had a run-in with your parents."

Someone who knew them, knew they had two young girls who would be alone with a teenage babysitter. He had to talk to people who knew the Howard family back then. Find out if Morris Clark was the only one involved, or if there were others.

Tess pulled out a chair and dropped into it. "I don't know who it could have been. Neither of my parents ever mentioned being at odds with anyone. Not in front of me, anyway. I do remember they became overly protective. I couldn't do some of the things the other kids my age did. They kept me on a very tight rein."

"I can understand that." And he could. It was hard for ordinary people to realize the evil that existed in their communities, sometimes masquerading as a trusted friend, but let it touch them or someone they loved, and they'd never forget. "We need to talk to people who knew them back then. Someone who would be around their age. Do you have family living here?"

"No. Both my mother and father were only children, and the extended families have about played out. I guess I'm the end of the line."

She didn't have anyone except a missing sister? That made it seem even worse. "All right, we need to start somewhere. What about this lawyer who thinks he's found Rhona? Why don't we go see him?"

"Frank Walpin? I guess that's as good a place to start as any. I'd like to find out if he's learned anything about this woman who claims to be her."

Neil got up, ready to go. "With both of us after him, we might get some information out of him."

In the car on the way over, Tess was quiet. He wondered what she was thinking. This had to be hard for her. After all these years a woman showing up, claiming to be her sister, when the family had never been able to find out anything, in spite of all their efforts. Adding this to the attempt on Tess's life, they were in a race against time. He just hoped she would realize she could trust him. It would make protecting her that much easier.

He pulled into the parking lot of the Davis and Walpin law firm, and Tess pointed to the sign. "I just realized he kept Herbert in the firm's name. That was nice of him."

"Or maybe good business," Neil said. "Herbert Davis was respected by everyone."

"There is that," Tess agreed. "We probably should have called ahead to make sure he's here."

The receptionist kept them waiting for ten minutes before ushering them into Frank's office. Neil noticed it had changed from the somewhat shabby but comfortable way it looked when Herbert was alive. He'd met Herbert shortly before his death and had liked the man, but he hadn't met Walpin. Which wasn't surprising. After all, he hadn't been here all that long, and from what he'd heard, a private detective wouldn't be important enough to associate with a self-important upper-level hotshot like Frank Walpin.

Since moving here from New York, Neil had tended to keep to himself most of the time. He hadn't completely come to grips with the events that had sent him looking for solitude and healing. Some things didn't just go away. It took time.

Heavy drapes of forest green linen framed the windows. The large walnut desk and comfortable chairs covered in dark green vinyl were new, and a magnificent seascape graced one wall, while walnut bookshelves filled the opposite one.

Frank nodded at them, but his expression was guarded. "Tess. What brings you here today?"

"We wanted to ask you something," she began, but Neil interrupted her.

"Tess received a troubling phone call. It was a tape of her sister as a little girl, crying for her mother. From what Tess says, her family got several of these calls after Rhona was kidnapped. We're wondering if there was a disgruntled employee or acquaintance who would have wanted to torture them that way."

"And you think I might know? Sorry, I was never a contemporary of theirs. I can't help you."

He turned his attention toward Tess, leaning forward, his lips curved in a smile, his gaze catching and holding hers. "I wish I could, Tess. You know I'd do anything to make this easier for you."

Neil didn't miss the way Tess shifted back in her chair, moving as far away from Frank as space allowed. Apparently she wasn't all that attracted to the guy. The thought pleased him more than it should have.

Tess tilted her chin a notch. "Herbert would have known."

Frank smiled. "But, Tess, darling, I have no idea what Herbert knew, and he's gone. There's no way we can find out anything now."

"No, but you can tell us about this woman who is claiming to be Rhona," Neil said. He'd had about enough of being ignored while Frank Walpin flirted with Tess.

Frank shot her a reproachful glance. "I asked you not to talk to anyone about that. We don't want to scare her away."

"Why would she be afraid to come openly?" Tess demanded. "Don't tell me she's afraid of me."

"No, it's not that. But there may be people who don't want the two of you together," Frank said. "After all, someone has kept her away from you for several years now."

"How did she get in touch with you?" Neil asked. It was about time a little information came their way. This was Tess's sister they were talking about. Or, at least, a woman who claimed to be Rhona Howard. Tess had a right to know what the attorney had done and the results.

Frank stiffened. "I would prefer to keep this information confidential until we can see how it plays out. The fewer outsiders we involve, the better it will be."

"Neil's not exactly an outsider," Tess said. "He's a private investigator I've asked to do some research into the kidnapping and what might have happened to my sister."

Frank's face flushed with anger. Neil narrowed his eyes. Interesting. He'd think help from any source would be welcome. So why did Frank care that a PI was on the job?

After a moment, when his complexion had faded back to normal, Frank said, "I fail to understand why that would be necessary. I'm perfectly capable of acting as a go-between for you in this situation."

"I'm sure you are," Tess said, "but Neil might run across something that would help. You said yourself we had to know for sure who she is. Like I pointed out earlier, DNA would help with that. I'd be happy to supply a sample anytime. And I want to run this through Child Search. We have people who are trained in this sort of work."

Neil sat back, letting her talk but still watching Walpin. He didn't like the way the guy avoided really saying anything. It was obvious that Frank Walpin seemed more interested in cozying up to Tess than giving them any useful information.

"When can I meet this woman? I'd like to talk to her face to face," Tess demanded. "And I want a name."

"You have to understand, she's been separated from her family and everything she knew for years. It's not always easy to go back. If we try to force her into anything, she might back off. She's extremely nervous about all of this. After all, we don't know where she's been or what she's been through the last twenty-four years. I'm betting it's been difficult, maybe even dangerous, for her."

Frank reached across the desk to clasp her hand, stroking it gently, as if no one else was in the room. "You know I'd do anything to bring this nightmare to an end. I'm working for you, Tess, trying to protect you. I want to make sure she's legitimate before I bring her into your life. And it's too soon to be talking about DNA. She's not ready for that. I think she's been hurt too many times, and it's hard for her to trust anyone. She feels like she's alone, no one to depend on. Give her a little time. Let's learn a little more about her before we push too hard."

Neil cleared his throat, and Tess whipped around to look at him. "Yes?"

He stood, towering over her. "I think we've learned all we're going to here. Maybe we need to leave, and let Mr. Walpin get back to work."

Tess stared at him, then looked uncertainly back at Frank before getting to her feet. "Yes, of course. I'm sorry we took so much of your time."

Frank smiled at her, still ignoring Neil. "You come by whenever you like. I'm always happy to see you. Perhaps next time we can have coffee or maybe go to lunch. I'd like to talk about some of this in private. Just the two of us."

Tess hesitated. "All right. Next time."

Neil held open the office door for her and put his hand on her shoulder, propelling her out into the reception room.

When they reached the car, Tess climbed inside and turned to face him. "What?"

"Is he always like that? I thought the guy was married."

"He is. He has been for several years. Why?"

"Because he was practically drooling over you back there. Does he act that way all the time?" As soon as the words left his mouth, he realized he'd gone too far. He should have let himself cool down before sounding off.

She shook her head. "Aren't you reading more into his behavior than was really there? I realize he's very friendly. It's just the way he acts."

And it wasn't any of his business? That's what her tone of voice seemed to imply. Well, she was wrong. He was involved in this mess, and he had no intention of backing down. "Then he needs to act more professional."

Neil drove out of the parking lot a little too fast and headed down the street. He wasn't jealous. Of course not. But, just the same, the thought remained although he tried to ignore it. He just wanted to protect her—do his duty as a citizen, and all that—but he knew an apology was in order. What she did really wasn't any of his business, and he was lucky she hadn't pointed that out to him.

He made an effort to sound contrite, although he was still rankled at Frank Walpin's behavior. "Okay. I'm sorry. Maybe I got a little carried away, but there's something about that guy that's easy to dislike."

Tess shot him an irritated look, and he got the impression she had a sharp retort ready. If so, she controlled the impulse. "I've been thinking of who might have known my father well enough to remember any problems he might have had with employees. Hank Branson used to run a filling station back then. He knew everyone in town. Maybe he'd know something."

"Okay, we'll look him up." He pulled into the parking area of the Country Kitchen. "It's almost noon. Let's get a bite to eat and kick around ideas. Make a list of people we can talk to. And that's another thing. You'd think Frank Walpin would appreciate all the help he could get, but he just flat out ordered us off the case."

Tess opened the car door. "Let it go. We need to concentrate on what we should do. Let him deal with the problems on his end."

She walked toward the restaurant, leaving him to trail along behind, feeling as if he'd acted like a fool. What was there about the woman that made him behave like this? Just the same, Walpin had been a shade too friendly. Did he want to solve this case, and return Rhona to her home, in order to win Tess's gratitude? Was that why he didn't want anyone else working on it?

Tess had almost reached the restaurant, and Neil walked faster so he could open the door for her.

● ● ●

Tess waved at Maxine, and headed for a booth by the window. Neil slid in across from her. "Okay, I admit I was out of line, but I still don't completely trust that guy."

She gave him a direct look, trying to make it clear how she felt. "I don't trust very many people right now, either. As for Frank Walpin, I'm hardly responsible for the way he behaves. He acts that way all the time. If it's all right with his wife, it's not my problem. We need to discuss what we're going to do. Not worry about Frank Walpin's personal behavior."

The waitress approached and Tess took the menu she offered, smiling up at her. "Hi, Maxine. What's good today?"

"Well, the special is chicken fried steak, and the chicken fried chicken is good, too. But if you're wanting healthy, we've got a great salad bar."

"I'm not into healthy right now," Tess said. "Eat and drink and be merry is my motto."

She shivered suddenly, mentally completing the rest of the quotation: Eat, drink, and be merry, for tomorrow we die. Why had she thought about that? Things were bad enough without her dredging up morbid sayings.

Maxine looked down at her with a concerned expression. "You okay?"

"I'm fine. I'll have the chicken fried chicken and iced tea." Tess handed the menu back and waited for Neil to order, trying to ignore the question in his eyes.

Maxine gave her an uncertain look, and nodded. "I'll be right back with your drinks."

Neil looked after her as she walked away. "Who's she? I don't remember seeing her here before."

"Her name's Maxine Crowley. I met her earlier, and she seems nice. I liked her immediately."

Neil had a bemused expression. "It's funny, she seems familiar in some way, but I'm sure I've never met her."

Because he'd have remembered? Maxine was pretty. All right, she was more than pretty—she was lovely—and she had a graceful way of moving that reminded one of a dancer. Tess was conscious of a prick of emotion that was too close to jealousy to be comfortable. Why should she care if Neil was interested in Maxine? It shouldn't concern her. Although she was depending on the man more every day, she still didn't know him well enough to be jealous of him. What was she thinking?

Neil buttered a roll and bit into it. "Okay, we know someone called you, and that tape he played had to have been made when you were kids. Since Morris Clark is in jail, who could have the tape, and who were the two men waiting for you out at the park?"

Tess pulled her thoughts back to the present. "I have no idea. It's starting to get to me. That phone call was hard to take."

"I know. I heard it, too." He took out a small notebook and a pen. "Who else can you think of who might have known your parents back then? Someone close enough to know who could have had a grudge against them."

"I've thought about Madge Paul. She was a friend of my mother, and women do confide in each other. We might talk to her."

"All right." Neil wrote down the name. "Who else?"

"I can't think of anyone just now. Maybe something will come to me later."

Tess noticed the man sitting two tables over. His back was turned to them but, from the rigid pose of his head and shoulders, she had a suspicion he was listening to their conversation. Probably she was mistaken, but she didn't feel like taking a chance. She nudged Neil with her foot. He shot her a startled glance, and she gave her head a little jerk toward the man, frowning and making a gesture to be quiet. Neil looked at the man and then back at her, and nodded. A moment later, he put his notebook away and made an aimless comment on the weather.

The man at the table rose and left, stepping outside and walking down the sidewalk. As he drew level with them, he turned his head and looked through the window, lips drawn back in a smile. Neil leaped to his feet and sprinted from the restaurant. Tess whirled around to stare after him. What had lit his fire?

A few minutes later, Neil returned and slid into the booth across from her. She looked at him, eyebrows raised, silently demanding an explanation.

He drew in a deep breath and exhaled. "That guy! He fit the description Andrea gave us out at Motel 6. His teeth even overlapped. He must have been registered there as Morris Clark. But if he was, we know he's lying, because Morris is in prison. I'm pretty sure that was one of the guys who tried to kill you."

A loud crash reverberated through the room.

Maxine had dropped a tray of dishes.

CHAPTER FIVE

Tess opened her eyes and stared around the shadowed bedroom. Something had jarred her awake. She lay still, body rigid, listening. There! A sound of movement came from somewhere in the darkened house. Carefully, she reached for the bedside phone. Easing the receiver up, she waited for the dial tone, relieved to hear the mechanical buzz. She punched in 911. A female voice answered.

"There's someone in my house," Tess blurted in a loud whisper.

"I'll get help there right away," the woman answered. "Give me your address, and please stay on the line until help arrives."

Tess gave her the information then left the line open while she reached for her cell phone, and quickly dialed Neil's number. He answered, sounding groggy. As soon as she heard his voice, she felt guilty for disturbing him.

"Tess? You okay?"

Of course he'd have caller ID. She should have known. "Listen. I'm sorry to bother you. It's just that someone is in the house, and you said to call—"

"Where in the house? Are you all right?"

"As right as I can be. I called 911, and I've got the dispatcher on the other line. I have to go."

"I'm on my way."

He hung up, and Tess picked up the telephone receiver again. A scream of sirens split the night. She heard a scrambling sound of someone running down the stairs. "The police are here," she cried into the phone. "I need to let them in."

She hung up the phone and grabbed a robe. Pulling it on, she ran for the stairs. Halfway down, she heard the slam of the back door. Tess paused, gripping the banister, realizing how foolish she had been. She'd been so intent on reaching the police knocking on her door she hadn't stopped to think of the burglar who was in the house with her. She hurried down the steps and ran to the door, yanking it open.

Chief of Police, Burke Palmer, stood there looking down at her. She'd gone to school with Burke, and it was a relief to see him, tall and blocky, with a take-no-nonsense expression on his face.

"Someone just went out the back," she gasped.

He turned around and made a motion with his hand, and a couple of the men with him jumped off the porch and ran around the house. Burke and Stanley Carson, another policeman, a friend of her father's, came in and quickly searched upstairs and down.

Tess sank into a chair, pulling the robe around her. Someone had been in her house. Even here she wasn't safe. Who was doing this to her? She listened to the policemen walking through the rooms, and wondered if the men outside had caught the intruder.

Burke and Stanley came back into the living room, and she looked at them with a questioning expression. "You didn't find anything?"

"Oh, I wouldn't say that. We didn't find anyone, if that's what you mean." Burke held out a length of rope in one hand, and in the other he held a wicked-looking knife. "We found these on the stairs."

Tess gripped the arms of her chair, staring at the rope and knife. A shiver of fear rippled up her spine. "On the stairs?"

"He was coming up to your bedroom, from the looks of it. Good thing you woke up. You been having any problems lately?"

"You could say that," she said, her voice shaking. "You might as well sit down. This will take a while."

There was a commotion outside, and then Neil burst through the door. "Tess? Are you all right?"

She half-rose out of her chair, then sank back down again. "Yes, I'm fine. Thanks for coming."

Neil glanced from her to the two policemen. "Burke, Stanley. What's going on?"

Burke nodded at him. "Neil. We got a call someone was in the house. When we got here, he'd left, but we found his calling card."

He motioned toward the knife and rope lying on the coffee table. Neil stared at them, and then at Tess. "He left those? Did you see him?"

She shook her head. He fumbled for a chair. "Okay, I think it's time to share what we know with the cops."

Burke nodded. "We were just getting around to that. So, let's get started."

Neil told them about the phone call and the incident at the park, Tess filling in the parts he missed. After they finished, Burke shook his head. "This sounds like a movie I watched last night. You want to tell me why neither one of you reported this?"

"I guess we were too busy concentrating on getting out of the park alive and wondering why anyone would be shooting at us," Tess said.

Neil spread his hands in agreement.

Stanley Carson spoke up. "I remember when you was kidnapped. You may not remember, but me and your dad went fishing together some. He was a good man. Losing you and your sister liked to have killed him. He sure was glad to get you back."

"Yes," Tess said, "but he never got over losing Rhona."

"No, that hurt him real bad. He never was quite the same after that. And he was having trouble with that guy he had to fire. Can't remember what his name was."

"Mr. Howard was having trouble with someone?" Neil leaned forward. "At the time the girls were kidnapped and held for ransom?"

"Yeah. Seems like he had more problems than he could handle right about then."

Burke Palmer eyed them quizzically. "You seem awfully interested in this guy, Neil. Why is that?'

"Well, the phone call. Tess recognized the tapes. They were played several times while she was young. So that made it seem personal, as if someone the family knew was trying to torment them. And since the tapes were of Rhona crying and calling for her mother, it seems logical to suspect the person playing them had access to her."

Burke stood. "I see. We'll take that into consideration. Since we can't do anything more here, we'll be on our way. If you have any more trouble, let us know. And it might be a good idea not to hold anything back from now on."

● ● ●

Tess saw them to the door, then came back to the living room. "Thanks for coming out in the middle of the night. I sort of panicked."

Neil looked at her, feeling a spurt of fear as he thought of what could have happened. "Reason enough to panic, I'd say. I'm glad you called me. I didn't care for the looks of that rope and knife. Isn't there someone you can stay with for a while?"

"No, there isn't. And I'd hesitate to ask anyone to put herself in danger anyway. I am going to have an alarm system installed, though. Just as soon as I can find out where to get one."

"I still don't like you staying here alone."

"Look, I'm not too happy about it either, but I can't leave. What if someone who really does have information about Rhona tries to call me? I have to stay where people can get in touch with me."

Right. Even if it meant putting her own life on the line. Arguing with her, though, would probably just make her even more determined to have her own way. He admired her spunk, but that stubborn streak could get her into big-time trouble.

Neil looked at his watch. "It's 3:30. I guess I'd better go and let you get some sleep."

Tess reached out and grabbed his arm. "Are you out of your mind? There's no way I can sleep now. How about some coffee?"

"Sounds good." He followed her to the kitchen, watching as she started a fresh pot brewing and chose cups from the cupboard. He suspected she wasn't as brave about staying here as she pretended to be. This was the second attempt on her life, and he had a feeling the two of them were running out of time.

"Tess, there has to be some reason these guys are after you. Maybe it's the will, and maybe it's something else."

"I've thought and thought, and it has to be something to do with the kidnapping and the will. There's nothing else." She sat at the table. "Trust me, I've led a very boring life. At least after I grew up."

"All right. Say it has to do with that. The phone call says it's linked to the kidnapping, because who else would have the tape? So we'll focus on that. Did your parents have a lot of money?"

"We weren't rich, but we always had enough, and the business has done well, but my father would have paid the ransom if it took everything he had."

"How much did they ask for?"

"Fifty thousand. Twenty-five for each of us. And then they took the money for Rhona and kept her. That's the worst part of all this. They kept her."

"Stanley said something about your dad having to fire someone right about then. You know anything about that?"

"No, but as soon as I can get to the office, I'm going to start digging back through the records, page-by-page, line-by-line, and if there's anything to be found, I'll find it."

"I think there's a link to the will, but I can't see what it could be. Where do you keep your copy?"

"Here in the desk. The original is with the attorney. You don't think someone could have seen it here do you? That would mean someone I know well enough to invite to my house is my enemy. I'd hate to think that."

"Well, it could be that, or it could be someone who came in while you were gone and looked around. Do you always lock your door?"

She sighed. "I'm not as careful about that as I should be. But it was locked tonight, and someone still got in. I can assure you it will be locked every minute of the day and night from now on."

"I'll get a guy over here to fix the window they broke to get in. If you don't mind me doing that. I'm not trying to take over, but I don't like the idea of someone breaking in while you're asleep. That alarm system is a great idea, too. I know a company that does good work. I can call them, if it's okay with you."

Tess grinned at him. "I don't mind a bit. In fact, I'd be happy for your help. I'll be at work all day, and it will be good to come home and have the window repaired. See if they can install the alarm today, too. I'll give you a key. Just be sure to give me the bill for the work."

• • •

Give him a key? She flushed at the implication, then told herself it didn't matter. He wouldn't think anything about it. In all the times they'd been together, Neil hadn't said anything out of line or made any effort to take advantage of the situation.

A part of her felt a little ticked at his apparent indifference toward her. Not that she wanted him to notice her, of course, and she probably looked a mess, wearing a ratty robe, her hair tangled and mussed from sleeping. Her traitorous mind played with the notion of how it would feel to have his fingers running through her hair. She gave herself a mental shake. Time to get back to business instead of sitting here dreaming of things she had no right to even think about.

Neil drained the last of the coffee from his cup. "Okay, I'll get on it as soon as Nate Talbot opens his shop. Look, Tess, there's something we need to talk about. This woman that Frank Walpin says might be Rhona. You need to meet her as soon as you can so we can do some checking. See who she really is, and learn where she's been. There are too many things happening right now. You've gone for twenty-four years with no news, and suddenly you're under attack and your missing sister is showing up?"

"Frank keeps putting me off, but now that the police know we're having trouble, maybe that will be enough to flush the woman who claims to be Rhona out into the open. I can't see any reason why she wouldn't want to meet with me, can you?"

"Not if she's the real deal."

"I don't want to prejudice myself against her before we have a chance to talk. She's been gone a long time, and there are things in her past we don't know about yet. For now, we'll let it ride and see what happens."

Tess glanced at the clock. Five a.m. "Would you like some breakfast? I could make blueberry pancakes and fry some bacon." And she liked the idea of eating breakfast sitting across the table from him. She kept telling herself to go slow, but her heart wasn't listening.

Neil pushed the notebook away from him. "I don't want to be a bother."

"No bother, and it would give me something constructive to do. I feel like one of those hamsters on a wheel, going around and around, and getting nowhere." She got out a cast iron skillet and set bacon to sizzling.

"I really can't see how we're going to learn anything. It's like trying to walk through a forest in the dark. We keep bumping into the trees. Things are happening, but we're not learning anything about who's doing what." She reached into the cupboard, brought out a green mixing bowl, and dumped in the ingredients for pancakes.

"Sooner or later, someone will make a mistake."

"I hope you're right." She set the griddle over the burner, and spooned batter onto the hot surface. "This will be done soon. Maybe we'll see things more clearly after we eat."

Neil left after breakfast, and Tess showered and went to work. She entered the plant, breathing in the familiar scents of sawdust and varnish. It seemed like most of her life had been spent here. She could run a saw, or choose upholstery fabric, knowing immediately which pattern would work best, and she'd worked hard to build trust and a good reputation in the business world.

Martha Oldman, the receptionist, greeted her. "Good morning. You doing okay?"

"Doing fine." Had word already spread about her break-in last night? "Anything I need to know about?"

"Dave has the designs ready for that line of reproductions you requested. Want me to page him for you?"

No, she didn't want that. She wanted to start looking at the old records, but business first. "Sure, send him in."

Dave carried a cardboard file into her office. "I thought you might need to see these, in case you have some suggestions to make."

"I'm sure you've done a good job, and I'm anxious to see the designs."

It had been her idea to create a line of antique reproductions based on the beautiful furnishings in her own home. Richard Howard had shared with his daughter his love for the elegant pieces from previous generations. She had been excited about this new line, but now her search for her sister overshadowed everything else. Rhona was the oldest. If she were here, she'd be the one in charge.

Tess had always felt like she had taken her sister's place.

She looked over the designs, liking what she saw. The pierced back splat of the dining room chairs was similar to, though not quite as elaborate as, the ones she had at home. The table was similar to designs from the Hepplewhite era, with a rectangular top and curved and splayed legs ending in brass paw feet.

Tess glanced through the other designs, finding them equally good. "These are great, exactly what I had in mind. You've done a fine job."

"Okay. If you approve, I'll meet with Josh, and let him see what we can work out."

He gathered up the pages and started to leave, then turned back. "I was coming home from Kansas City—we'd been to a Royals game—and I saw police cars at your house. Everything okay?"

Tess hesitated, and then decided it wasn't a secret. "I had a break-in last night."

Dave sat back down. "You okay?"

"I guess. The police found a knife and a rope on the stairs. Neil Vaughn is having an alarm installed for me today."

"You serious?"

"I'm afraid so."

"Look, Tess. Maybe you need to stay somewhere else for a few nights. Mildred would be happy to have you stay with us."

Tess shook her head. "I'll be all right. The police will keep an eye on my street, and I'll have the alarm. But thank you."

"Well, if you change your mind, let me know. You tell me if you need help. And if you don't tell me, I'll sic my wife on you."

Tess laughed. "Don't do that. I'm afraid of her."

Dave grinned and stood. "I don't blame you. I'm a little afraid myself."

After he left, Tess spent the best part of the morning searching the employment records from her father's time, but with no luck. Several people had quit and some had been fired, but nothing indicated anyone bore animosity toward her father. No name from the past had any meaning. Of course, she'd been a child then. No doubt her parents had talked about things to which she'd never paid any attention. She'd make a list of people who used to work here and talk to them. Maybe one of them would come up with something.

She closed the ledger and leaned back in her chair. It was two o'clock, past time for lunch, and she needed to eat something. Maybe a little fresh air would help her think better. She was groggy from lack of sleep and sitting still for too long. She'd take a break, go to the Country Kitchen for lunch, and maybe then she'd be more alert. Either that or take a nap at her desk, something she'd been fighting all morning.

Tess strolled into the Country Kitchen and took a seat in a window booth. The restaurant was practically deserted, the lunch crowd long gone. Maxine brought her food, and then, after looking around the room, slid in across from her.

"Look, I'm not trying to meddle, but I overheard what Mr. Vaughn said, that someone had tried to kill you. Was he serious?"

Tess reached for a roll, tearing it in half. "I'm afraid so, and someone broke into my house last night. The police found a knife on the stairs, so apparently someone is still trying."

Maxine stared at her, the blood draining from her cheeks. "Are you all right?"

"I'm fine, but it was a little scary there for a while." That was putting it mildly. She had been terrified. This was the second attempt on her life, and she hoped there wasn't another one lurking in her future.

Maxine leaned forward. "I hear a lot of gossip here. People never realize how their voices carry. They say you were kidnapped when you were young."

Tess placed her fork on her plate, and sipped water before answering. This wasn't anything she wanted to talk about, but everyone in town knew the story. She might as well tell the truth.

"Yes, me and my older sister. My parents paid the ransom. They got me back, but the kidnappers kept Rhona. We never saw her again."

"That's terrible. Did your family try to find her?"

"They did everything they could. As long as they lived, they never gave up. They paid out a fortune on private detectives, and they started a foundation to help find missing children. Finding Rhona consumed their lives." She thought of her mother in her last days, still grieving, refusing to accept the truth that her daughter might not come back.

Maxine used a napkin to wipe a drop of water from the table. "And you? How did you feel?"

"Like part of me is missing, and I'll never rest until I find her. I don't know what's going on, but it's possible it might be tied to that kidnapping. I keep hoping that, if she's out there, she'll try to get in touch with me. I miss her, and I want her back." Tess wiped her eyes, overcome with emotion.

Maxine reached over and took her hand. "I hope you find her. I'm sure she misses you, too."

"If she's out there, why doesn't she call or try to get in touch? I'm afraid something's happened to her, and I don't think I could bear that." And it hurt to think that the woman who might be her sister would go to an attorney instead of trying to reach family.

"Don't think that way. Keep hoping, keep believing, and one of these days when you least expect it, she'll come back to you."

"I hope you're right. And I won't give up. I'll keep trying to find her, and praying God will give her back to me, but it gets hard sometimes." Tess blinked back tears and grabbed a napkin to blot the ones she couldn't control.

"You pray about it?" Maxine asked.

"I've prayed for her every day she's been gone. It's the first thing I think of in the morning, and the last thing at night."

Maxine's eyes sparkled with tears as she gripped Tess's hand. "I have a feeling those prayers have kept her safe. You keep right on trusting and praying. Put it in God's hands, and leave it there."

The door opened, and a couple of women entered. Maxine got out of the booth and stood beside it for a moment before reaching out and patting Tess on the shoulder. "I have to get to work now. But I'll keep my ears open. Maybe I'll hear something that you can use. You never know."

She moved away and Tess, her appetite gone, paid the bill and left. When she reached her car, she paused, looking up at the clear blue sky. Rhona? Where are you? Come home or call me. I want to find you, but I don't know what to do next.

She sat in the car for a minute before driving back to the office. There had to be something in those files she'd overlooked. She would pack them up and take them home with her, and if there was a reference to any problem her father had with anyone, she'd find it. She couldn't give up. Someone somewhere knew something about her sister, and she wouldn't quit until she'd exhausted every lead.

CHAPTER SIX

Neil leaned back in his office chair, thinking about Rhona Howard. All these years with no sight of her, and suddenly she just gets in touch with an attorney? Why not call Tess direct? There were too many unanswered questions, and he was involved in this investigation whether Frank Walpin liked it or not. Neil refused to think about why he was so determined to protect Tess, other than doing what any decent man would. He just was. That was enough for now.

He reached for the phone and called Bob Gorman, who had worked with him on several cases and had been looking at the information on Tess and her sister. "You busy right now? I need to run something by you."

"Something about the Howard girls?"

"Yeah, we've had a strange thing come up."

"Okay, I'm on my way. I'll be there in five minutes."

While Neil waited, he did another search on Richard Howard, Tess's father. There wasn't much, just some of the same information he already had about the kidnapping. Mentioned he was owner of Howard's Manufacturing, and that was about it.

Bob opened the door and walked in; big, dependable, with red hair, green eyes, and a handful of freckles scattered across his cheeks. He was the first person Neil met when he moved to Cedar City, and had turned out to be one of the best friends he'd ever had.

"That didn't take long. Where were you?"

"At the Country Kitchen, having coffee. You seen that new waitress, Maxine?"

"Yeah, I was in there with Tess. Why?"

"I tried to get a date, and I saw yes in her eyes, but she said no."

"That's hard to believe." Neil grinned. "I guess you'll have to keep trying."

"I intend to. Now what's going on? I've gone over those Internet files until I'm cross-eyed, talked to a few people around town, but so far I haven't found a thing."

"Here's something you don't know. Frank Walpin came to see Tess. It seems a woman who claims to be Rhona Howard has been in touch with his office. He says he's checking her out to make sure she's the real thing before he lets them meet. But Tess is curious about why the woman went to a lawyer, and why she's so reluctant to meet the sister she hasn't seen for twenty-four years."

"Tess is smart. Always was. Doesn't it seem a little strange that there's all this interest in Rhona Howard all of a sudden. I mean all this time, and now, Bam! Stuff is popping up all over the place."

"Yeah." Neil hesitated for a minute, not sure if he should divulge the contents of Mrs. Howard's will, but he trusted Bob, and if they were going to work together he couldn't keep him in the dark.

"What?" Bob demanded. "I know you well enough to know you're holding something back. Let's have it."

"It's just that Tess showed me her mother's will. It divides the property evenly between her two daughters."

Bob sucked in his breath and then heaved it out again. "I knew Doris Howard. She never gave up on finding Rhona. But what if she never shows up? What happens to the money?"

"Rhona's share is in a separate account, drawing interest. If she never shows up, then it goes to Child Search. But get this. If Tess dies first and Rhona comes back and proves who she is, she inherits her share and Tess's share too, in payment for all the years she's been gone."

Bob's eyes narrowed in concentration. "You know what? You've just given someone a good reason to kill Tess. And there's a woman who has already met with Frank Walpin and established her claim as Rhona Howard. I'd say Tess is in trouble."

Neil nodded. "I know her mother meant well, but she's set Tess up to be a victim, and I'm coming around to thinking that's what that ambush in the park was all about. The question is, how could they have learned what's in the will?"

"That's what we have to find out. Any ideas where to start?" Bob asked.

"Not a clue, but we're both going to have to do some serious digging on this one. I have a feeling we've got the deck stacked against us. But for Tess's sake we have to tie this thing together. Her life may depend on it." And maybe in the process they would discover why someone had made the effort to include him.

"I'll get busy. In the meantime, you keep me in the loop so I'll know if I need to look in a different direction." Bob got to his feet. "I'll call you tonight just to check in, say, around eight?"

"That'll work. I hope one of us comes up with something." And they needed to find it as soon as possible. Whoever was behind these attacks was doing a good job of hiding their tracks.

"One more thing, what do you know about Frank Walpin? Is he from around here? Does he have a good reputation around town? Anything you can think of?"

Bob shrugged. "Actually I don't know much about him. I'm not important enough to chum around with Frank. He's upper level society. Or at least he thinks he is. Why?"

"It just seems odd he doesn't bring this woman to Tess and let them meet. Why keep holding her off like this? She's pressed him to introduce them, but he always has some reason why the time isn't right."

"I see what you mean. That does seem odd. Maybe we should do some checking on him. No telling what we might find. I have heard he has an eye for good-looking women."

"I'm not surprised." Neil thought of the way Walpin had acted toward Tess. Yeah, he could see him playing the field. Not that it helped them with their current problem. "I'll do some digging in his past. I'll let you know what I find out."

"Right. See you around. And it wouldn't hurt to say a prayer or two. We need all the help we can get."

Bob left, closing the door behind him, and Neil stared at it, thinking. Both Tess and Bob went to church, and they each had a strong faith. Yes, he was a Christian, but just talking to them made him aware they had something he didn't have.

He reached for the phone. First he'd call Stanley and set up a meeting. There were some questions he needed to ask.

Burke answered. "Sorry. It's Stan's day off. He's out at that farm of his, getting ready to put up a second cutting of hay next week. I'll give you his cell phone number."

Neil wrote down the number and then called. "Hey, Stanley. You going to be home for a while? If you are, I'd like to bring Tess out and talk to you."

"Sure, that'd be just fine. Like to see that girl again. Maybe the three of us can come up with an idea who's after her."

"Okay, soon as I pick her up, we'll be on our way."

He hung up and called Tess. "Since it's Saturday, are you up to driving out to Stanley's and talking to him about your dad?"

"I guess so. When?"

"Now, if it's okay. I told him we'd be right out."

"I'll be ready."

When he got there, she was waiting on the porch, wearing jeans again and a light blue T-shirt, her golden hair flowing to her shoulders. Just watching her walk toward the car brought a smile to his face. She was becoming an important part of his life, and he wasn't sure how he could prevent it from happening. Wasn't sure he wanted to prevent it, although he knew it would be a mistake. Knowing someone wanted to hurt her brought all of his protective instincts rushing to the fore.

Please, God, help me to keep her safe. He stopped in surprise. Had he prayed? It had been a long time since he'd done that.

Tess got in the car and smiled at him. "This is a good idea. Stanley was friends with my dad. Maybe he can tell us something."

"It's worth a try. How do you like your alarm system?"

"I love it. I make sure it's turned on before I go to bed, and I sleep great. In fact, this morning I overslept. I can't remember when I've done that."

Yeah, having someone shoot at you and drop a knife on your stairs while you were sleeping would do that. It was surprising she'd managed to get any sleep after all that had happened.

He pulled up to the town's only stoplight, waiting for it to turn green. "One thing I've wondered about. You said your parents hired private investigators. Didn't they find anything at all? Back then, the clues would have been fresher. Now we're looking at a very cold case."

"No, if they had, I'd have known. No one ever turned up anything."

"Wonder why Morris Clark is in jail? That's something we can check into, see where he lived when he was arrested. Maybe we can find out something there."

He turned onto the lane leading to Stanley's house, driving past the large cedar trees standing sentinel on each side, right inside the gate. The cattle guard rattled behind them, and he could see a herd of Hereford and Angus cows grazing in the distance. The lane led through an overgrown pasture dotted with goldenrod and wild sunflowers. Soon as they had a frost, the leaves would start to turn from green to red, bronze, and gold. He liked fall in the Ozarks, and the land around Cedar City was full of hills and hollows. The sky today was blue as only an October sky could be, just a handful of small clouds floating overhead.

Stanley's home was a white farmhouse with a porch across the front. A black-and-tan hound dog came around the corner of the house to greet them, and Neil reached down to scratch its ears. The dog wagged its tail and followed him as they walked toward the porch. The screen door opened and Stanley stepped out, grinning.

"Don't mind old Rattler there. He likes company."

"Is he always this friendly?" Neil asked. "Not much of a watchdog."

"You're wrong on that. He's a great watchdog. Watching is what he does best. Of course it's all he does, but at least he's good at something." Stanley held the screen door open, letting them pass but blocking the dog that showed every inclination of coming too.

"No, you stay outside. You know you're not allowed in here." He looked at them expectantly. "So, you got anything to tell me?"

"Nothing new," Neil said. "We wanted to ask you about Tess's dad and the guy you said he fired."

Tess sat in the bentwood rocker. "Anything you can tell us will help. As far as I know, Dad never found out anything about Rhona, but I was a child. Did he say anything to you?"

Stanley sat in a wooden straight-backed chair, and tipped it until the front legs were off the floor. "Nothing I can remember. I know he was all tore up about it, and we didn't do a lot of fishing after that. He just didn't have the heart for it. Losing you girls liked to have done him in. And then, when he didn't get Rhona back, well, it just about finished him off. He never was the same after that."

Tess nodded. "It destroyed our family."

Neil saw the sorrow in her face, and it strengthened his resolve to discover the truth. She'd been through too much to have to endure any more. Of course, keeping her safe had to be his main concern. "Stanley, you said Richard had to fire someone. Do you remember anything about it?"

"Not a lot. It happened so long ago that it's hard to remember the details. I believe his name was Clyde something. I do know it had to do with stealing. Seems this Clyde was swiping supplies from the plant, and he got caught."

"So he got fired. Did Dad turn him over to the police?" Tess asked.

"No, I don't think so. Your dad was a decent sort. He wouldn't want to cause unnecessary trouble for anyone. Just fired him. Made the guy mad, from what I heard. He made some threats, but then he left town. Anyway, about then you girls disappeared, and Richard had other things on his mind."

"And then I came back and Rhona didn't."

Neil was stunned by the guilt and shame in her voice. Did she believe it was her fault her sister was missing? That might explain why she was so determined to risk her own life to find Rhona.

Stanley must have picked up on it too, because he said, "Now don't you go thinking that was your fault. You was just a baby, four years old. There wasn't nothing you could have done, one way or another."

Tess managed a crooked little smile that made Neil want to take her in his arms and comfort her. He might have done it too, if Stanley hadn't been there. He was starting to realize what a heavy load she had carried all these years. She would never be free to live her life fully until she knew the truth about what had happened to her sister.

Stanley lowered his chair until all four legs were on the floor. "Tell you what. You talk to Madge Paul. Her and your mother was good friends. She might know more than I would. Women talk about things more than men do."

Again, Tess nodded, still looking too solemn to suit Neil.

"Have you got any leads on who broke into Tess's house the other night?" he asked.

Stanley shook his head. "Not a thing, but it's not from lack of trying. My guess is that it's the same bunch that tried to shoot you out at the park. We talked to Andrea out at the motel, but she couldn't tell us much more, except she gave us the license number of their car."

"She did? I should have asked her for that." How could he have slipped up on something so elementary?

"Wouldn't have done you any good. We found the car. It'd been stolen down in Arkansas. We traced it to the owner, but the police there didn't know any more than we did. Just that the guy who owned it had reported it stolen."

Tess sighed. "Everywhere we turn, we hit a dead end."

There had to be something Neil was overlooking, and he had to find it before anything else happened. He couldn't fail this time. The memory of Rebecca lying in the casket at her funeral still haunted him.

"Don't give up, Tess," Stanley said. "You got a good police force working on it, and you got this private investigator and Bob Gorman. We're not going to let you down."

"I know." Tess smiled. "I appreciate everything you're doing, but I just keep feeling like I have a target painted on my back, and someone is aiming at the bull's-eye."

"It does seem to look that way," Stanley said, "but you're not alone. We're keeping an eye on you, and God's watching out for you, too. You got Him on your side, and that's better than a whole army."

Neil listened, thinking here was another strong Christian. If he hung around with these people all the time, maybe he'd find his way back to the fold. He glanced over at Tess. "You got any more questions?"

She shook her head. "Nothing I can think of. Are you ready to go?"

"If you are. Thanks, Stanley. If you hear anything you can tell us, I'd appreciate it."

"I'll do the best I can. Of course, I can't give you confidential in- formation from the police department, but anything I can share, I sure will."

Neil rose to his feet, and held out his hand to Tess. "Come on, I'll walk you past Rattler the watchdog."

She chuckled and took hold, letting him lift her up. As their hands met, a powerful surge of awareness leaped between them, startling Neil. He could tell by the surprised glance she gave him that she'd felt it too. Suddenly he was feeling a longing all too familiar to him. A longing he never expected to experience again.

Stanley watched them with a twinkle in his eyes. "I'll be seeing the both of you around town. You take care now."

"Yeah. Be seeing you," Neil responded absently, still holding Tess's hand. He should turn loose, but he didn't. Somehow he had to distance himself emotionally from Tess Howard. A woman like her deserved better than he could give her.

On the way back to town, Tess was quiet, staring out the windshield as if she had something on her mind. Finally she started talking. "I said that Rhona being gone destroyed our family." She glanced over at him. "I know other people can't see that, but it's true."

"I'm sure it had to affect you in ways outsiders can't understand."

She turned her head, looking out the side window. "My parents always sort of fell apart on her birthday. It got worse every year."

"Did they celebrate your birthday?" He hoped so. How could they not, after all she'd been through?

"Yes, of course, but no matter how hard they tried, there was a shadow over our celebrating. We were all too conscious of the one who wasn't there. And they tried to make Christmas good for me, but there was always a certain sadness lurking under all the Christmas spirit. If it hadn't been for their friends from church who always rallied around, especially then, I don't know what they would have done."

He didn't know how to answer that, but just for an instant he had a glimpse of what he'd been missing. "You've been through a bad time, haven't you?"

"No more than a lot of people, I guess, but it happened to me. That makes a difference I suppose."

"It makes a big difference. When other people have trouble, we can be sympathetic and do all we can to help, but we're always on the outside, not able to feel the pain. When it happens to us, we have to live with it." He knew from experience when trouble hit personally, it could be devastating.

Tess pressed her lips together, blinking back tears. "And when it happens to us, we're the ones locked in with the pain and the darkness, with no one to help us except God. I credit my parents with helping me strengthen my own faith over the years. And now, I'm being attacked again."

"Don't give up. We're going to see this through, and we'll follow every lead no matter how slim or where it leads. Trust me on this."

She reached over and placed her hand on his arm, and he felt that same awareness of her touch flowing through him again. He didn't understand how she could have this effect on him, but being with her brought back feelings he thought were dead.

"I appreciate all you've done. With you on my side, I feel like I have hope."

Neil covered her hand with his, wishing he could do something to ease her pain. He pulled into her driveway. "Why don't you look through those records again for someone named Clyde? Maybe he didn't have anything to do with it, but then again, maybe he did. We won't know until we talk to him."

"All right, I'll do that. Thanks for taking me with you to see Stanley, even if we didn't learn much." She opened the car door and got out, and he did the same.

"I'll walk with you." He wouldn't leave until he knew she was safe inside the house and the alarm was working.

She smiled up at him. "You don't have to do that."

"I want to."

They climbed the steps and stopped. Tess gripped his arm as they stared at the 8x10 brown envelope with her name on it, leaning against the screen door.

CHAPTER SEVEN

Surely it was nothing. Just something a friend or neighbor had dropped by and, not finding her home, had left it for her, but the onslaught of recent events had set her nerves on edge, causing her to see menace on every corner.

Neil picked up the envelope, turned it over, and looked at the back before raising his eyebrows questioningly. "Are you expecting anything?"

Tess shook her head, staring at the envelope. "I don't have any idea what it could be."

He took her arm, and she fought the urge to lean closer, realizing how grateful she was that he was there. In spite of her determination to not get involved, she was depending more and more on him, something she didn't have the right to do. When this was over, he would walk away and she would be left alone, the way she had been left alone when her sister wasn't returned, or when her parents died. That's the way it had always been. Everyone she loved gone, leaving her behind. Why should she expect it to be different this time?

He removed the key from her hand and unlocked the door, ushering her inside. "So, the kitchen again?"

"I suppose so." She followed him, afraid to open the envelope, afraid to ignore it. What had happened to her? She was the strong one, the rock her mother had depended on the last years of her life. How could a woman so used to being in control have a life that was falling apart?

Neil sat down, placing the envelope on the table. "You want me to open it?"

"Please." Tess forced herself to relax, to loosen muscles wound tight by tension. He opened the flap, reached inside, and pulled out photographs, large ones, 8x10.

He placed the first one on the table, facing her. She stared in disbelief at the enlarged picture of her getting into her car, which was parked in front of Neil's office. She darted a look at him, mouth open in surprise. The second picture showed her unlocking her own front door. She grabbed the envelope, looking for information about where it had come from.

"Look at this one," Neil said.

The third picture showed Tess sitting at her kitchen table in exactly the same chair where she sat now. Since it was a little blurred, it must have been taken through the kitchen window. She surged to her feet and rushed to yank the curtains closed, shutting out any intruders.

"They took my picture in my own house? What do the others look like?"

He placed number four on the table, and she leaned over to get a good look. "That's me coming out of the Country Kitchen. They're stalking me. I'm not safe anywhere."

"It looks that way. Have you noticed any strangers following you around?" Neil asked, looking worried.

Tess shook her head, not trusting herself to answer without falling apart. Someone had been taking pictures of her just going about her life. Somehow that made it seem more sinister. She wasn't doing anything to threaten anyone or put herself in danger—just living her life—and they were stalking her.

"What's the next one?" she asked, not really wanting to see, but knowing she had no choice.

Neil placed it on the table. "It shows you in the parking lot of your office."

Tess recognized the suit. "That's what I wore to work Wednesday." She took another look at the other photos, pointing to the one of her leaving his office, and then to the one of the Country Kitchen. "These two were taken on the same day. I'm wearing the same jeans and shirt in both of them. So someone watched me leaving your office, and followed me to the restaurant. And I never even noticed. How could I have been so blind?"

"Because you weren't expecting anyone to creep around after you taking pictures. But we'll both be more on our guard now." He placed the sixth and last photo down in front of her. "This one is of both of us."

Tess stared at the picture of the two of them going into Frank Walpin's office. She drew a long breath and puffed it out. "What do these people want from me? Who are they, and why are they harassing me like this?"

Tess slapped a hand over the picture of her in the kitchen. That one bothered her the most. After she'd installed the alarm, she'd felt safe. Apparently that wasn't a luxury she dared indulge in. "It's a good thing they didn't use a high-powered rifle instead of a camera. I'd be dead." She glanced at Neil. "So what do we do now?"

He pulled out his cell phone. "Now we call the police. We're not keeping any more secrets from them. Someone is playing rough, and I can't watch you all the time. We've got to have help."

Tess bristled. "I don't expect you to watch me all the time! I'm perfectly capable of taking care of myself."

"I didn't intend to imply that you weren't, but it doesn't hurt to have another pair of eyes on the job. That's all I meant."

She glowered at him, knowing she was overreacting, but she couldn't help herself. Those pictures scared her. After he finished his call, he walked around the table and pulled her up to stand beside him. His arms went around her, cradling her close against him. She rested her head on his chest, reveling in the warmth of his arms, the security of his embrace. The violence they were facing had drawn them so close she realized they were becoming more than just friends, and that scared her.

Tess pulled away, stepping out of his arms, even though every thought, every heartbeat, longed to stay enclosed in that warm embrace. She had to keep her mind on the goal. She tilted her head back to look up at him. "I appreciate all you've done, but I have to do what I can to protect myself. After all, like you said, you can't be there all the time."

He started to say something, but a knock on the door drove them farther apart as Tess backed away.

"That's probably the police," she said.

"Probably so." Neil stepped around her and walked to the front door.

She listened to the sound of male voices coming her way. Burke Palmer entered the kitchen with Neil. "Hear you got something we need to look at."

Tess pointed at the table. "These were in that envelope, leaning against the front door when we got here. I have no idea where they came from."

"Well, let's have a look." He stood with his hands loosely clasped behind his back, gazing stolidly at the photographs. "I don't like this."

"I don't like it much, myself," Tess said, humiliated by the quiver in her voice. She pulled herself together and made eye contact with him. "Are you having any luck finding the person harassing me?"

"No, not yet." After a few moments, Burke slid the photographs into the envelope. "I'll take these with me, if you don't mind."

"I'll be glad to get rid of them. They give me the creeps."

He glanced at Neil. "You ever get in touch with Stan? What was that all about?"

"We wanted to ask him if he remembered the name of that guy Tess's dad had to fire. He came up with a first name—Clyde. That ring a bell with you?"

Burke shook his head. "Not at the moment. I'll ask the guys at the station and see if any of them knows anything. What about employment records. You find anything there?"

"Not so far," Tess answered, "but I brought them home with me for a second search. You know this all started with that note holding out a promise of information about my sister. Then a woman gets in touch with Frank Walpin, claiming to be Rhona."

"I want to make a copy of that will. I'll give it back to you, but I want to take a second look at it, just to try to figure out what we're up against."

She removed a thick envelope from the desk and handed it to him. "I'll talk to people who knew my parents, and see if I can learn if anything disturbing happened before we were kidnapped."

"Good idea. Let me know what you find out. In the meantime, I'm going to do a better job of tracking you. Someone got close enough to take these pictures. That's too close for comfort."

After the men left the room, Tess walked over to the window, pushed the curtains aside, and stared out, lips clamped shut. The person responsible for the pictures didn't know it, but he had lit a fire in her. She was determined to find him and put a stop to whatever game he was playing.

• • •

Neil showed Burke out, then went back to the kitchen. Tess was standing by the window, staring out.

Reflected in the glass, her expression turned thoughtful, and he paused, wondering what was coming. She turned around and looked at him. "Stanley mentioned praying. What about you, Neil? Are you a praying man?"

He stood silent for a moment then shrugged. "I used to be, but something happened that made me back off. It seemed to me that God didn't really care what happened to me or to the people I loved."

Her eyes widened. She asked the question he'd been dreading. "Do you want to talk about it?"

No, he didn't. This was a part of his life he never talked about. It's why he wasn't a cop anymore. But, for some reason, he walked around and sat down at the table. Tess sank into a chair across from him, waiting.

After taking a minute to steel himself, Neil started talking. "I was an undercover policeman investigating the mob in New York. During the investigation, I met a woman who was a potential witness. I started out seeing her just to find out what she knew, but it didn't stay that way for long. I fell for her. Fell hard."

Tess watched him, and the compassion in her blue eyes almost unnerved him.

"She had information that could be crucial to our case, but she was afraid to talk, knowing they'd come after her if she cooperated with the police."

Talking about it brought memories he'd tried to forget, but somehow it also brought a sense of relief.

Tess waited, not saying anything.

"I promised I'd protect her if she would testify. I wouldn't let them get to her. By this time we were engaged. I gave her a ring, but she couldn't wear it openly because it might jeopardize our case. The defense could claim a conflict of interest."

Tess reached out to clasp his hand, and he let his fingers twine around hers. They sat that way for a moment, and then he sighed and tightened his grip.

"She agreed to testify. Even came in for an interview. I took her home and drove away. They were waiting for her inside the house. They killed her."

"It wasn't your fault," Tess said.

"It was my fault. If I hadn't talked her into testifying, she'd still be alive. She knew it was dangerous, but she loved me, and I'd promised she'd be safe. I betrayed her. After the funeral I quit the police force, left town, and became a private investigator."

"And you ended up here. Why?"

"I'd traveled all over and couldn't seem to settle down anywhere. The memories of Rebecca wouldn't leave me alone. Finally I came here, and met Bob. He talked me into staying. He's been a real friend, and I'm starting to get my life back to normal."

"You've been through a lot. I had no idea. And now you've been saddled with my problems."

"I want to do everything I can to help you. I let Rebecca down. Somehow, if I can save you, it might make it up to her in some way."

She was silent for a moment, and he had a feeling he had upset her, although he didn't know why.

"So that's what turned you against God?" she asked.

He nodded. "It seems to me, if God really cares about us, He'd have saved Rebecca. She was trying to do what was right. So was I. And He let some slimy scum murder her."

"God doesn't always perform a miracle just because we want one. Was Rebecca a Christian?"

"Yes, she was. So why didn't He help her?"

Tess took her time answering, and he had a feeling she was searching for the right words. "I don't think we can blame God for the bad things that happen. The man who killed her had freedom of choice. He chose to kill. God didn't make him do it."

"I know all of that, but I can't forget what happened."

She looked straight at him, eye to eye. "You'll never forget, it's part of your life, your history. But we have a choice to make, too—choose to let it destroy us, or choose to turn loose of the guilt and the grief, and move on. "

Neil released her hand, and got up from his chair. He placed his palms on the table, leaning over. "What about you, Tess? How good are you at letting go?"

Not waiting for an answer to his question, he walked out of the kitchen, closing the front door behind him, not bothering to look back.

CHAPTER EIGHT

The phone rang just as Tess was finishing breakfast. She stared at it, waiting for the answering machine to pick up, afraid it might be another recording of Rhona's voice. There hadn't been any more of those dreadful calls, but a shiver of fear raced through her every time she heard the phone ring.

Frank Walpin's voice came over the line, and she grabbed for the receiver. From the tone he used and the way he snapped out his words, he was extremely angry about something.

"Hello? I'm here, Frank."

"I just had a visit from the police concerning the woman who claims to be Rhona. I told you not to tell anyone, and apparently you've broadcast it to everyone in town." Gone was the flattering, slightly condescending manner. "Would you like to explain why you are trying to sabotage this investigation?"

"I didn't go to the police." Tess said firmly. "They came to me."

There was silence for the space of three seconds, and then he asked, "What are you talking about?"

"Someone broke into my house, evidently planning to kill me."

"Evidently? What does that mean?"

"It means that I called 911. When the police arrived, whoever was in my house ran out the back door. He left his knife and a piece of rope on the stairs for the police to find."

There was more silence on the other end of the line. She waited.

When Frank spoke again, he sounded shocked, but he was still angry. "I had no idea. But I still can't understand why you would tell the police about a very sensitive investigation, knowing it could jeopardize the outcome. The woman claiming to be your sister couldn't possibly be part of what happened to you. In fact, she's not even in Cedar City right now. But if you keep blabbing all over town about her, you could be putting her in danger. And there is absolutely no reason to involve the police in this. After all, she hasn't committed a crime. She's a victim, just like you were. Give her a chance, Tess. Keep your mouth shut until I can work this out."

"Since this was the second time someone tried to kill me, I thought it would be foolish to hold anything back. And now that you've brought up this woman who claims to be my sister, I want to meet her."

And he might as well understand she wasn't planning to take no for an answer. This had gone on long enough. He was either going to produce this woman or—well, Tess wasn't sure what she would do if he refused, but at any rate, she'd do her best to run a bluff.

"You will meet her. Eventually. Just trust me, Tess. I only want what's best for you."

His voice had slipped into that smooth, smarmy tone that she found so irritating. She could understand how Neil felt. This man would be easy not to like. After all, he had a wife, and while Tess didn't care that much for Gloria, getting involved with a married man wasn't her style.

"Eventually won't work. I want to meet her now."

"That's impossible."

Okay, the anger was back. Why was this so important to him? She had a hunch he wasn't used to being crossed. Did he just want his own way? Or was there some other reason he was so determined to keep them apart?

She held firm, refusing to be intimidated. "I don't think so. You arrange a meeting now, or there won't be one."

His voice changed again, becoming less belligerent, more soothing. "I understand how you feel, Tess, but these things take time. If you'll just be patient until I do a little more investigating, I'll set up a meeting."

"You don't understand. I can't see any reason for us not to meet. If she really is my sister, I'd think she would want to see me. If meeting a family member she hasn't seen in twenty-four years isn't a high priority for her, then perhaps she isn't my sister."

And that really was the crux of the matter. She wanted to see her sister, would move mountains to get to her. It hurt to think this woman who just might be Rhona would call an attorney as a go-between, and would delay the meeting.

"Of course she's your sister. Don't be unreasonable, Tess, darling."

"In the first place, I'm not your darling. And in the second place, how can you be so certain she's my sister and then tell me you have to do some more investigating in order to be sure?"

"I mean that I'm about eighty percent certain she's your sister, but not quite one hundred percent. I want to be completely convinced before we go any farther. Surely you can understand that."

"Let's see if you can understand this. I want to meet her no later than tomorrow. And I want Neil Vaughn present at the meeting."

Depending, of course, on whether Neil would be willing to meet with them. She hadn't heard from him since their disagreement. She'd been thinking over what he'd said, and realized they both had guilt to resolve. Although she hated to admit it, she wasn't all that good at letting go, either.

"That's impossible," Frank snapped. "I insist on this meeting being entirely confidential."

"Without me, there won't be a meeting. I told you my requirements. You either agree to them, or I won't meet with her. It seems strange to me that she would be so reluctant to see me. After all, I am her only living relative."

"Very well, if you insist. I'll speak with her and set out the terms. If she's agreeable, I'll get back to you."

"See that you do. I'm tired of being pushed around, and I'm definitely tired of someone trying to kill me. I want to get to the bottom of what's going on, and I want to do it now. And let's be clear on one thing. I will insist on using DNA to prove that she really is my sister."

"Like I said, I'll get back to you."

There was a sharp click, and Tess was left listening to the dial tone. She hung up the receiver and sat staring into space, thinking. First she had to mend fences with Neil, and then she had to ask him if he'd be at the meeting with her supposed big sister.

She thought about that for a minute. Was all of this hassle setting her up to reject this woman before she ever met her? Just because she was ticked at Frank, and upset at the attacks and harassment, was no reason to make up her mind that the woman was a fake before they had a chance to meet. She needed to be very prayerful about this, trusting God to lead her to make the right decision.

Tess changed into tan pants and a cream-colored silk blouse. If she wanted to mend fences with Neil, it would take more than a phone call. She needed to apologize in person. And she had to get her emotions under control. He'd made it clear that he was only helping her in an effort to atone for failing Rebecca. Considering that she didn't need any distractions right now, that should have been comforting, but it only left her feeling rejected.

She drove the short distance to his office. While she was right in believing that Neil needed to let go of what had happened, he was right, too. She had lived in the past for too many years, but recognizing the problem was a lot easier than finding a solution.

She parked in front of the building and got out, fighting a growing case of nerves. Apologizing never came easy for her, and having to humble herself was difficult. She hated to think it, but maybe God was teaching her an important lesson: she needed help from others in order to survive, no matter how hard it was to accept.

The parking lot was empty except for his SUV. Perhaps they wouldn't be interrupted until she had finished talking to him.

• • •

Neil was on the phone when Tess opened the door and walked in. She gave him a tentative smile, as if she wasn't sure of her welcome. He raised his eyebrows, but otherwise ignored her while taking notes and asking questions of the person on the line. He had an idea why she was here. Probably he should have made the first effort to solve their disagreement, but he had been trying to deal with the memories talking about his past had revived. Telling Tess about Rebecca had brought it all flooding back. Losing her had damaged him in ways that could never be repaired. He was a different man now, one he didn't always like.

He finished the call and looked at her. "Morning."

"Good morning. I need to talk to you."

"Oh, what about?"

She flushed, and he felt a stab of guilt. She had enough to worry about without him giving her trouble. He also knew she'd been right, although he hated to admit it. It was time he tried to let go of the past. He'd carried it around with him far too long. The problem was, it still hurt. Still woke him up at night, destroying all chance of sleep. Guilt was a difficult emotion, and talking about turning loose was a lot easier than actually doing it.

"About what happened at my house. I realize I was out of line to say what I did. I do think you'll have to let go of what happened in the past before you can heal, but you were right about me, too. I'm not very good at letting go, either. We each have some problems to deal with, but that shouldn't get in the way of us being friends."

He nodded his agreement, noticing her relief. "You're right. We each have some past baggage holding us back. Moving on is tough."

"I know. To be truthful, I don't think I can begin to let go of anything as long as I'm in danger. And there's this woman who claims to be my sister. That keeps me rooted in the past."

"Have you set up a meeting yet?"

"That's the second reason I'm here. Frank Walpin called. He was upset because the police had been to see him about this woman. I got a little angry, too, and insisted on seeing her no later than tomorrow. But I don't want to meet with the two of them without someone there in my corner. You have experience interviewing people. I'd like to hire you to meet with us."

He squinted at her. "You want to hire me? Why not just ask me to be there as a friend?"

"I wasn't sure you'd want to help me after I upset you, and besides, I don't like to impose on you. I'm not used to asking for help."

Yeah. He'd noticed. But it was time she got a few things straight. "Okay, let me make something clear. No, you can't hire me. I'll be at the meeting as a friend. I'm in this until we find out the truth, Tess. I want you to understand that."

Tears misted her eyes. She sat looking at him as if a great load had slipped from her shoulders. Her voice held a slight tremor. "I'd be so grateful. I'm afraid my emotions will get in the way. I don't want to accept someone who's working a scam, but at the same time, I don't want to reject a woman who could be my sister."

"I'll be a trained outsider, just watching what goes on. Is that what you want?"

He'd be watching very carefully. He still thought the woman showing up like this was just a little too much of a coincidence.

Someone had to be there for Tess, and he was glad she had come to him. He never knew Rhona or any member of her family, so he wouldn't be able to spot common traits, unless it was something she shared with Tess, but after his years with the police, he was good at reading body language and figuring out if someone was lying to him. Most of the time.

The familiar fragrance of her perfume drifted to him, and he breathed deeply, something sweet and spicy, like her. He wanted to reach out to her, comfort her, tell her it would be all right, but he had learned it would be a mistake to promise something he might not have the power to deliver. Life didn't always turn out the way one wanted.

"Yes. Your honest opinion. That's all I want." She made a move to get up, but he stopped her.

"Don't rush off. I've been thinking about that guy who runs the filling station. Do you have time to go see him today?"

"I suppose so. When do you want to go?"

"What about now? Do you know where he lives?" The sooner the better, as far as he was concerned. He wasn't sure Tess realized how vulnerable she was, but he'd had too much experience with the seamier side of life. These people were determined to get rid of her.

Tess gave him a smile, a real smile, the first one she'd been able to dredge up since entering the office. "Of course I know. He's one of my favorites. First I'll need to call the factory and let them know I won't be in for a couple of hours. I don't have anything pressing to take care of right at the moment, so it's no problem. Am I driving or are you?"

"I'll drive, you give directions." He stood up, pushing his chair back. "If you're ready, let's go."

● ● ●

As soon as they were seated in the SUV, Tess fastened her seatbelt and turned to look at him. "Have you heard anything from the police about the break-in or the pictures?"

He drove out of the lot and onto the street. "Nothing yet. Have you?"

"No. I hoped we'd have heard something by now."

"There may be a break in the case before long."

Tess stared out the windshield. It would be nice if she could stay alive until they got that break. Right now, she wouldn't bet on it either way. She gave directions to Hank Branson's house, and they stopped in front of an old-fashioned bungalow. The house sported what looked like a fresh coat of white paint. The immaculate yard had recently been mowed, and an ancient pickup sat in the driveway; it, too, was spotlessly clean.

Tess grinned at Neil. "Hank's always been a bit of a perfectionist. He ran the only service station in town that had a clean restroom."

He laughed, and opened the car door. "I hope his memory is as good as his housekeeping."

Tess knocked on the door, and it opened. A frail elderly man, stooped with age, smiled broadly. "Well, if it isn't Miss Tess. You come right on in here and let me look at you."

Tess gave him a hug. "Hank, it's good to see you. How are you?"

"As well as can be expected, I guess," he said. "You doing all right?"

"I'm fine." She glanced over at Neil. "Do you know Neil Vaughn?"

"That private investigator fellow? Never met him, but I've heard about him." He reached out to shake Neil's hand. "The two of you come in here and sit down. I'm guessing you got something on your mind."

"Well, yes, you could say so," Tess said, not sure where to begin. She glanced helplessly at Neil, and he came to her rescue.

"We have a problem. Tess got a note asking her to go to Coffman Park at eight o'clock one night from someone who was supposed to have information about her sister. I got a call telling me there'd be someone at the same place, same time, who had information about a case I was working on. We both showed up in separate cars, and we got shot at."

Hank stared at Tess. "You all right? They didn't hurt you?"

"I'm fine, but that's not all. A few nights later, someone broke into my house. I called 911, and the police found a knife and a rope on the stairs." Just talking about it sent a shiver through her. If she hadn't woke up and called for help, she'd have died in that upstairs bedroom.

Hank's mouth dropped open as he stared from her to Neil. "My stars, girl. Someone's got it in for you. Wonder who it could be?"

"We think it might be connected to the kidnapping. Stanley Carson used to fish with Dad. He says there was some trouble over a man who got fired right before Rhona and I were taken."

Hank nodded. "It caused a real stink. Richard caught that guy stealing him blind. He fired him. If I remember right, after he was fired he made some threats around town. I'd have thought he had a hand in taking you girls, but I believe he'd left before it happened."

Neil leaned forward, drawing Hank's attention. "Do you remember the name of the man? Stanley thought it was Clyde, but he couldn't remember a last name."

Hank nodded. "That's him all right. Clyde Perkins. A real piece of work he was. He ought to have been fired. Nothing but a common thief."

"Is there anything you can tell us about the kidnapping, or anyone who was suspected of being guilty?" Tess asked. "Anyone besides Morris Clark, I mean."

"Well, the cops suspected Clyde, of course, and seems like there was someone else. Just can't remember who. But then it turned out that Clark guy was the one who snatched you girls. So I guess Clyde didn't have anything to do with it."

Neil rose to his feet. "We appreciate this, Hank. It gives us a name to go on. It's the only thing we've got so far."

Hank stood and hugged Tess. "You take care of this girl for me. She's a good one."

Tess hugged him back. "You're special to me, too."

He followed them out to the porch, and watched as they drove away.

Tess turned to face Neil. "Well, that wasn't much help. We've got a name, but if he'd already left town, I can't see how he could be involved."

"How do we know he left town? If the guy was making threats, why would he leave without at least trying to get even?

Tess stared at him, "What do you mean?"

"He could have been in hiding someplace, and people just thought he was gone."

"But he didn't do the kidnapping. Morris Clark did. How does this Clyde fit into the equation?"

"I don't know, but I'm going to run a check on him. Maybe he's one of the men trying to get rid of you now. And maybe there were more people involved than you knew. After all, you were only four years old."

She couldn't remember anyone except Morris and Aggie, but she had been a terrified child. How far could she trust her memory? "So what we do now?"

"Now we go back to the office and get on the computer. If this guy has a record, we'll find him."

Neil parked in front of the office, and they went inside. Soon he was clicking through sites, looking for the name Clyde Perkins. A few minutes later, he brought up a new screen, and Tess sucked in her breath. There on the monitor was a picture of the man who fit the description Andrea at the motel had given them. Even to the overlapping front teeth.

CHAPTER NINE

Neil pointed at the monitor, recognizing the flabby face, the overlapping teeth, the thinning hair. "That's him! It has to be."

What's more, that was the man he had chased from the restaurant. The man who had been listening to them talk. He had jumped into a white car and disappeared around the corner before Neil could catch him for questioning.

Tess erupted in fury. "That's the man who shot at us? Probably the same man who got into my house with a knife? You mean that's the man my father fired, and now he's back causing trouble for me? Why? I've never done anything to him."

Neil glanced up at her, noting the flushed cheeks, the eyes bright with anger, and was glad her temper wasn't directed at him. "Do you remember him?"

If anything, his question only infuriated her all the more. "No, of course I don't remember him. I've never seen that man before in my entire life." She hesitated, suddenly looking unsure. "Not that I remember, anyway."

Would she remember? Four years old, snatched from her home, held in a strange place. She'd have been terrified. Could they trust her memory? Neil clicked through the site. Clyde Perkins had a rap sheet, mostly petty crime. He'd done a couple of years for extortion. Nothing in the site showed a connection to Morris Clark. So did Clyde take part in the kidnapping, or had he run across the crime online and decided to use what he'd learned to make a profit?

Neil printed off the information, making four copies: one for him, one for Tess, one for Bob, and one for the police. He handed Tess her copy and leaned back in his chair, scanning his own pages.

"I can't see that this helps much." Tess looked up from reading and shrugged. "What now?"

"How about going to meet that woman you mentioned? Madge something." He could go by himself, but she might be more willing to talk if Tess was along.

"Madge Paul, my mother's best friend. That sounds like a good idea. Let's go."

Neil followed her to the car, thinking that at least they were going through the motions of investigating. Whether they would learn anything remained to be seen. He got in and reached for his seat belt. Tess sat beside him, alert, bright-eyed. She'd been through a lot, but it seemed each experience just made her more determined to see this through. The longer he knew this woman, the more she fascinated him.

She settled back in the seat. "Turn to the right down at the corner. I'll tell you where to go from there."

Neil glanced at the rearview mirror. After the photographs Tess had received, he tried to keep a closer watch, knowing that the stalker was still out there and might use something more dangerous than a camera next time. Following Tess's directions, he pulled up in front of a gray ranch-style house with black shutters.

Tess reached for the door handle. "I hope she can tell us something."

Neil followed her up the walk. They stepped onto the small concrete stoop, and he rang the doorbell. They waited, but no one answered. From somewhere inside came the barking of a dog, sounding almost frantic.

A woman hurried across the yard. "I'm Letha Collins. Are you looking for Madge?"

"Is she home?" Tess asked.

"I'm not sure. I haven't seen her for a couple of days. Usually she comes over for coffee in the morning, but she just hasn't shown up. I've tried to call her, but she doesn't answer."

"Maybe she's gone on a trip."

The woman shook her head. "She wouldn't go away without asking me to take care of Cricket, her little dog. I keep him when she goes to her daughter's in Kansas City."

Nothing about this sounded right. Neil turned to examine the door, and noticed scratches marring the gray paint of the door frame. Someone had jimmied the lock. He took his handkerchief out of his pocket and wrapped it over the doorknob. The knob turned beneath his hand.

He backed up. "I think we need to call the police."

Tess looked bewildered. "The police? Why do we need them?"

"Because we can't go barging in on our own. If anything has happened to Mrs. Paul, it would be better if we don't interfere in a crime scene."

"A crime scene?" Mrs. Collins exclaimed, starting toward him. "Madge is my friend. I'm going in there."

"No, ma'am," Neil said as gently as he could. "It won't hurt to wait a few minutes. This might be a job for the police." He pulled out his cell phone and dialed, ignoring the angry woman. Tess didn't look happy with him, either, but he'd deal with that later. He wished they'd come to see Madge Paul earlier, because he had a hunch they were too late.

A police car pulled up at the curb, and Burke and Stanley approached. Burke shook his head. "Every time I hear from you, it's trouble. What is it this time?"

"Madge Paul. Mrs. Collins hasn't seen her for a couple of days.

The dog sounds like he's frantic, and it looks like someone has tampered with the door." Neil pointed out the scratch marks and then stepped out of the way.

Burke opened the door and yelled, "Mrs. Paul? It's the police."

Nothing.

He and Stanley walked inside.

Stan came back in a few minutes with a small white dog nestled in his arms. "Keep him out of the way, will you? Maybe get him something to drink. I think he's thirsty."

Letha Collins reached out for him. "Come to me, Cricket. It's okay. You're all right now." She glanced at Neil and Tess. "I'm going to take him over to my house, but I'm coming back. If something has happened to Madge, I have a right to know. She's a good friend."

Neil waited with Tess, wishing he could spare her from what he feared. Burke and Stanley were taking too long for just a routine search. Tess must have felt the same way, because those gorgeous blue eyes were full of misery.

• • •

Tess watched the door, waiting for Burke to come back. What were they doing in there? Why didn't at least one of them come to the door and tell them what was going on? She glanced at Neil. "Remember when we were in the Country Kitchen and that man, Clyde Perkins, was sitting there, listening? Didn't we mention Madge then?"

He stared at her for a moment then nodded in agreement.

"He could have found out where she lived and done something to her." She hoped not. If so, it would be her fault. She was the one who had mentioned Madge Paul might know something about the kidnapping.

Letha came back and stopped at the foot of the steps. "Have the police said anything?"

"No, not yet," Tess said, and if they didn't show up soon, she was going inside, whether Neil liked it or not. This woman had been her mother's best friend, someone Tess had known all her life. Madge had always kept a jar full of snickerdoodle cookies, knowing they were Tess's favorites. She couldn't bear it if something had happened to Madge.

There was the sound of footsteps, and Burke appeared in the open door. "We've called people in to process a crime scene. I'm sorry, but you can't come inside. We have to avoid contaminating evidence as much as possible."

Tess sucked in her breath. Crime scene? "Is Madge in there?"

Please, God let him say no.

Burke nodded, eyes full of compassion. "She's here. But she's dead."

"How?" Tess forced the words out through lips gone cold with shock. "What happened?"

"Someone broke in. Looks like they overpowered her, and smothered her with a pillow. It's still over her face."

Tess's stomach clenched. She was afraid she'd be sick.

Letha moaned, and Tess took the woman's arm and led her a little way from the house. "Are you okay?"

Letha looked dazed. "Madge! No! No, it can't be."

Tess put her arm around the grieving woman. "Why don't you go home, and I'll come over later and tell you what happened?"

Letha pulled away from her. "No! I need to stay here. She would do the same for me."

Madge must have been sixty-five or older. No way could she have put up much of a fight against Clyde Perkins, if he was the one who had attacked her. Tess didn't have one bit of proof, but she had a feeling this was the work of whoever had tried to kill her. She'd just been luckier than Madge. Tess slid her arm around Letha's waist, and they stood, linked together, heads bowed in prayer, each determined to stay there until Madge had been moved from her home.

Letha drew a shuddering breath. "I'm going to keep Cricket. He's got a home with me as long as he lives. That's the least I can do for her. She thought a lot of that little dog. He's going to miss her something terrible."

Tess fought a lump in her throat. At least Madge had a dog. She hadn't made room in her life for anything that would hinder her search for Rhona.

Suddenly she felt incredibly lonely. She glanced at Neil, and he gave her a reassuring nod, as if he knew what she was thinking. He had moved into her life like a whirlwind, and in spite of her efforts to keep him out, he had become a special friend. More than a friend.

But he was still in love with Rebecca. How could she compete with a dead woman?

● ● ●

Other police arrived, and Neil recognized the county coroner. He glanced at Letha Collins and Tess, knowing the wait was agony for them.

Someone had murdered Madge Paul in her bed. He stepped out of the way as four policemen carried a stretcher past him. Inside the body bag, he could see the outline of a slight form. A rush of anger whipped through him. No woman that small could have defended herself against someone determined to kill her. He had a feeling Madge had been murdered to keep her from telling what she remembered about the Howard girls' kidnapping, and what their mother had told her in confidence.

Burke came out to talk to them. "Okay, let's have it. What are you doing here?"

"We found a picture of Clyde Perkins online, and then we decided to come over and ask Madge what she remembered about Tess and Rhona being kidnapped. We arrived and found that she hadn't been seen lately, and there were scratches on the door. We called you. That's all we know."

"Ah-huh!" Burke grunted. "Who's Clyde Perkins?"

"He's the guy Tess's father fired a few days before the girls were taken, and he's also the guy who registered as Morris Clark out at Motel 6. We think he might have heard us talking about Madge."

Burke Palmer's lips tightened, his face red with sudden anger. Neil didn't have any trouble understanding why. If he were in Burke's place, he'd be angry, too.

"Look, we didn't intend to withhold information. We just learned the name of the guy Tess's dad fired. And we just discovered what we know about Perkins about half an hour ago. I would have told you, but we just hadn't got around to it."

"You hold back information from me again, and I'll run you in for obstructing an investigation."

"I'm sorry," Tess said. "Like Neil said, we didn't intend to keep anything from you. We just found out these things. We'd have told you everything we knew."

"Yeah, when? Whenever you got around to it? I'm warning the both of you, pull this again and you'll regret it. Now get out of here. I'll want to talk to you later."

He turned his back on them, and addressed Letha Collins.

Neil took Tess by the arm and led her to the car. "Let's go before we rile him even more."

She glared back at Burke, but she got inside and pulled the door shut. Neil walked around to the driver's side and slid in behind the wheel. "It's almost noon. How about getting something to eat?"

"I'm not hungry."

"Maybe not. But you need to eat something." He pulled away from the curb and headed downtown.

Tess didn't look happy, but at least she didn't protest when he pulled into the parking lot of the Country Kitchen. They found an empty booth. Maxine waited on them, and they sat silent until she brought their food.

Neil pushed the basket of rolls over where Tess could reach them. "Eat. We've got a fight on our hands. You're going to need your strength."

She glared at him, but he noted with satisfaction she broke a roll in two and smeared it with butter.

He waited until she had actually taken a couple bites of the excellent baked chicken before bringing up something he'd thought of on the way to the restaurant. "When we were going over the files I printed out about you and Rhona, you said something about two men that police had suspected, but they had the wrong names. Who were they?"

She stared at him, looking thoughtful. "I'd forgotten that. I'll look it up as soon as I get home."

Her cell phone rang and she took the call, just listening to the caller for the most part. Finally she said, "That's fine. I'll be expecting you.'

Tess closed the phone, and Neil looked across the table at her, eyebrows raised. Her hand trembled as she reached for her water glass. "That was Frank Walpin. He and the woman who claims to be Rhona will be at my house at two o'clock tomorrow afternoon. Can you be there?"

"I'll try to get there by one-thirty, in case they're early."

Maxine was clearing dishes off the table across from their booth. Now she paused and looked their way. "You're meeting with your sister? The one who was stolen at the same time you were?"

Tess licked her lips, then took a long drink of water. "The woman who claims to be her. I don't know for sure who she is."

"I see." Maxine stacked a couple of plates on the tray. "I'll be praying." She glanced at Neil, and then looked back at Tess. "I'm glad he'll be there with you. You can trust him." She hefted the tray of dishes and walked back to the kitchen.

Tess sighed. "Now that it's come, I'm really nervous. I hope it's her, but a part of me is afraid it's not."

Neil reached over and took her hands in his. He wasn't worried about meeting Frank Walpin and the woman. He was worried about Tess spending the night alone in that empty house.

CHAPTER TEN

Tess walked the floor, glancing at the clock. One-thirty. Frank and the woman would be here in thirty minutes. She'd been walking and praying all morning, unable to sit down or relax. Could her search really be coming to an end? Was this woman her long lost sister? Or was it just someone trying to take advantage of the situation?

The doorbell rang and she paused, catching her breath. Could that be Frank? This early? She hurried to the door and opened it to find Neil smiling at her.

"You doing okay?"

"I guess, but I'm glad you came." She reached for his hand.

He gently tightened his fingers around hers, and smiled. Flustered, she let go and stepped back. "Come on in. They should be here before long."

They entered the living room and she looked around, wondering if the woman claiming to be Rhona would see anything familiar. More to the point, would there be anything about this person that would be familiar to her?

The doorbell rang again, and Tess shot a pleading glance in Neil's direction. He nodded, comfortingly. "You stay here. I'll let them in."

She waited, forcing herself to relax. Voices sounded, and soon Frank entered the room, followed by a blond-haired woman. Neil brought up the rear.

Tess stared at the woman, wanting to believe, but afraid to trust too soon. The woman wore her hair straight and hanging past her shoulders. Her makeup looked professional, not just thrown on in a hurry the way Tess usually did. Her tan pants and coral knit top emphasized her trim figure. Tess sighed. Nothing about this woman seemed familiar, but of course it wouldn't. She had been unrealistic to even imagine a thirty-year-old woman would have anything in common with a six-year-old girl.

She stood as Frank approached.

"Tess, I want you to meet Rhona Howard. She's been looking forward to meeting you."

The woman held out her hand, and Tess mechanically reached to take it. She was meeting a stranger. Nothing about this woman reminded Tess of her sister. This wasn't at all the way she had imagined them greeting each other. She motioned toward the chairs. "Let's sit down and visit."

Even to her own ears, Tess sounded stiff, unwelcoming. That wasn't the way she wanted to come across, but she couldn't force herself to relax. Rhona, if that was her name, smiled at her, but she didn't say anything. Tess waited for someone to break the silence, then decided it was up to her to speak first.

"Where have you been all this time?"

"I've lived in several places." The woman pointed at the painting of mountains hovering over a log cabin. "I remember that painting, and the fireplace. I used to sit in front of it, drinking hot chocolate."

Tess remembered that too. A ray of hope dawned. Maybe she really was Rhona. She glanced at Neil, who was sitting back in the brown recliner, looking relaxed, but she knew him well enough by now to realize he was really watching intently, looking for anything that might be out of line.

"We have some catching up to do, a lot to talk about," Tess said.

"That's for sure. One of the things we need to discuss is that I'm not called Rhona anymore. Aggie always called me Erin. It's the name I'm used to."

She didn't want to be called by her real name? The name her parents had given her? Tess thought about it, and decided it might be better this way. She wouldn't call her Rhona until she was sure this really was her sister. "Is Aggie still alive?"

Erin shook her head. "No. She's been gone for some time."

"Did they keep you all these years?" Was that why she never called home? Perhaps they wouldn't let her get in touch with her real family.

"Well, yes, why wouldn't they?" Erin's eyebrows rose as if she was surprised anyone would ask a question like that.

"Were they good to you?" Tess couldn't bear it if they weren't.

Erin's mouth dropped open. "I can't believe you asked that. Of course they were good. Aggie was like a mother to me."

Tess stared at her, not sure how to respond to this. They had kept Rhona away from her own family, and she didn't resent it? She remembered the way her parents had grieved, the way they had never reconciled to losing her. Didn't this woman have any idea how they might have felt?

"We never gave up on finding you. Dad died six years ago, Mom's been gone two years in March." Would she care? This meeting wasn't going the way Tess had hoped.

Erin sighed. "I didn't know that. Somehow I always thought they would be here when I came back."

"Why didn't you come earlier?" Tess heard the faint note of accusation in her voice and regretted it, but she wasn't very good at hiding her feelings. Surely, in twenty-four years, she could have called at least once.

Erin glanced down at her hands folded in her lap, then looked up again to meet Tess's eyes. "I wasn't sure I'd be welcome."

"Not be welcome?" Tess stared at her, not believing this. "How could you think that? My parents died grieving over you."

My parents? She probably should have said our parents. That was a slip of the tongue.

"I'm sorry. I suppose I should have called. It just never seemed the right time."

Tess glanced from her to Neil and Frank, then back again. "Then why are you here today? After all this time, why now?"

Frank answered before Erin could say anything. "It seemed like a good time. After all, neither of you have anyone. You need each other."

Tess stared at Erin, trying to see something, anything, that reminded her of Rhona or any other family member. Her hair was blond like Rhona's had been, and like Tess and their mother. She was built like their mother, fairly tall and slender. All of that made it appear possible that this could be her sister, but there was still a good reason to be careful, not too quick to jump to conclusions. A little proof would be good right about now.

"We need time to get acquainted. How about having lunch together tomorrow at the Country Kitchen, just the two of us?"

Frank started to protest, but Neil interrupted him. "That sounds like a good idea. You need some private time to catch up."

Erin glanced at Frank, then smiled at Tess. "I'd like that. What time?"

"Say eleven thirty. Get in ahead of the rush."

Maybe if they sat down and talked, just the two of them, they could find some common ground. Tess supposed it was natural for them to be stiff with each other at first. If they could relax over lunch, it would be better than sitting here with Frank and Neil watching every move.

Frank looked at his watch. "I have an appointment in twenty minutes. I think this has gone well for a first meeting. We'll be in touch, Tess." He waited as Erin rose, and then he took her arm, leading her toward the front door. Again, he ignored Neil, who followed them then closed the door and locked it before coming back into the living room.

Tess looked at him, wondering if he could see how helpless and let down she felt. From the compassion in his eyes, she was sure he did. Having him there was the only thing that made the situation bearable.

• • •

Neil sat down, and smiled at Tess. "You all right?"

"I guess so. That didn't play out the way I hoped."

"This is just the first meeting. You'll both be more relaxed the next time. Getting together for lunch is a good idea."

Tess glanced helplessly around the room. "I have dreamed about this meeting for years. I guess I expected too much."

"Well, you've been separated for a long time. There's bound to be a little stiffness at first."

"My head knows you're right, but my heart isn't listening. I wanted something positive, something I'd recognize."

She blinked back tears, and he ached for her. He'd like to tell her something positive, but they hadn't learned enough at this meeting to make a decision one way or another. He'd learned his lesson, though. As soon as he left here, he was going to talk to Burke. He wasn't planning to withhold information again. Burke was a good guy, a good policeman, but he took his job seriously, and he could get hot if he found out people were holding back something he needed to solve a case.

First, though, Neil was going to check with Bob, who had been stationed across the street to take pictures of the woman as she arrived and left.

He watched Tess for a minute, seeing her downcast expression. She'd been through so much, and even though she had doubts, she must have had hope that there would be something to prove that this woman was really her sister.

"Look, don't give up. This was just a first meeting. Maybe the next one will go better."

Hope dawned in her eyes. "You think there's a chance she might be Rhona?"

"I'm just saying take it slow, trust in God, and give Erin a chance. And remember this, you're not alone. I'm here."

She gave him a tremulous smile. "I know, and I appreciate it. I don't know what I'd do without you."

"I'm here as long as you need me."

She looked more relaxed now, not so beaten down. Her eyes were bright, and she wasn't clasping the arms of her chair so tightly. A few more minutes, and he'd feel more comfortable about leaving her alone.

She glanced at the row of family pictures on the mantle with such a sad expression he hurt for her. Finally, she looked at him. "Thank you for coming today. It meant a lot to me."

He smiled at her. "Thanks for asking me. I'm here, Tess, anytime you need me, call and I'll come."

"I know," she said softly, her eyes bright with unshed tears. "It's been a long time since I've had someone to rely on."

No, she'd been the caregiver, the person in charge, the one who had to be strong. No wonder she was wearing down. He wished he could do more to help her, but the best thing he could do was find the people who wanted her dead.

Tess squared her shoulders. "I'm going to spend the rest of the afternoon going through those records to see what I can turn up."

"That sounds like a good idea. Do you need me for anything else? If you don't, there's something I should do."

She took a deep breath and then shook her head. "No, I can't think of anything."

He stood and smiled at her. "I'll get back to you later today. Why don't you record your impression of Erin and this first meeting in your notebook, while it's fresh in your mind?"

She nodded. "Good idea. You do the same. I'd like to compare them."

"Yeah, we need to do that. I'm sure we noticed different things. I'll call you and let you know when I'm coming."

She followed him to the door, and he heard the lock click behind him. He was glad she was taking every precaution. Nothing could keep her safe from someone determined to get to her, but at least she wasn't making it easy for them.

Once in his car, he called Bob. "You get any pictures?"

"Got some good ones. I've already downloaded them in my computer and sent them to you. That what you wanted?"

"That's it. How about meeting me at the police station. I want to talk to Burke and after the dressing down I got earlier, I'm not inclined to hold anything back."

Bob laughed. "Good idea. I'll head on over. Burke can get a little upset if he thinks someone is interfering in his investigation."

"Yeah, I know. See you there."

Neil drove out of Tess's driveway and headed for the police station. He didn't know what good it would do, but at least they'd have the cops working on it with them. He parked in front and got out. Bob pulled in and parked beside him.

Burke was standing by the front desk and talking to Floyd Hankins, the dispatcher, when they walked in. He turned and gave them a straight look.

"What brings you two here?"

"Got something to show you and talk about," Bob said.

"Ah-huh. Well, come on back, and let's get started." Burke led the way to his office and sat down behind the desk, waving them toward a couple of chairs. "What've you got?"

Neil sat down and started talking. "Tess insisted on meeting this woman who claimed to be her sister. Frank Walpin brought her by the house today. She's tall, blond, good-looking, and calls herself Erin. Seems that's the name Aggie Clark gave her."

"Yeah? How did Tess take that?" Burke asked.

"From her expression, not too well, but she didn't say much. They were both a little stiff, which I guess is to be expected, considering how long it's been since they've seen each other." Neil thought back to the stilted conversation that had taken place in Tess's living room. "They're meeting tomorrow for lunch at the Country Kitchen. Maybe it will go a little better then."

"You think this woman is really Rhona Howard?" Burke asked.

"I don't know. Bob was across the street taking pictures. He brought them along to show you."

Burke turned his attention to Bob, who handed him his digital camera. "I've downloaded them into my computer and sent a copy to Neil. I'd have sent you one, but I don't have your email address."

"Huh. I'll have to see you get it." Burke took the camera, and called a young woman into the room. "Here. See if you can download these pictures."

Neil watched the woman leave and then turned back to Burke. "Is there any way we can find out for sure if this woman is who she claims to be?"

"Well, there's DNA. We could check it against Tess, and see if we can get a match."

Yeah, but he thought it was a little early for that. They'd just had one very short meeting so far, and hadn't learned much one way or the other. Besides, he had a hunch Frank Walpin would object if they brought it up right now. The guy seemed a little defensive. "Tell you what, let's hold off on that. Give Tess a chance to talk to her. If she thinks this Erin is her sister, then we'll ask for a DNA sample."

"Sounds good. I appreciate you both sharing this with me. If you get onto anything else, I'd like to know it."

Neil stood up and nodded at Burke. "We'll do it. I just want to find out the truth before these guys strike again."

"We all want that," Burke said. "Keep in touch."

Neil and Bob left, walking outside to get in their cars. "Where are you going now?" Neil asked.

"I thought I might stop and get a cup of coffee," Bob said. "Why? Do you need me for anything?"

"No, just curious. I suppose you're drinking your coffee at the Country Kitchen."

"Where else? I think I'm making progress, too. She kind of acts like she's glad to see me, and she's getting friendlier."

Neil laughed. "Well, hang in there. Maxine's a beautiful woman. Maybe she's starting to notice your good qualities."

"And I have so many." Bob grinned and got in his car.

Neil watched as he drove out of the lot. He had a feeling old Bob was hooked. He hoped Maxine felt the same way, because Bob was a great guy, one of the few people Neil trusted enough to share personal problems. The first friend Neil had made in Cedar City, Bob had done everything he could to help him set up his offi ce and get his new business off the ground. That kind of friend didn't come along every day. He'd hate to see the guy get hurt.

Neil got into his own car and headed toward his office. Halfway there, he noticed a white car following him. He kept an eye on it, but when he reached the office, the car passed on by. He dismissed the prickling of apprehension as nerves, and went inside.

He worked for a couple of hours, trying to catch up on the cases he was supposed to be working. The phone rang several times, but when he answered, no one was there. The number on the caller I.D. wasn't familiar to him, but the calls were so irritating he finally stopped answering them, letting the machine take them. He was worried about Tess, wondering how she was doing. Finally he phoned her, and when she answered, she sounded down.

"Hey, how are you getting along?"

"All right, I guess."

He thought fast. "I'm coming over, and I thought I'd stop and pick up some take-out. What would you like?"

Silence. He waited. "Tess?"

"Yes, I'm here. I've got some lasagna in the freezer. I'll put it in the oven, and it should be about ready when you get here."

"Sounds good. You want me to stop and get some garlic bread?"

"No, I've got a loaf of that too."

"Okay, be there in a few minutes." He hung up the phone, thinking this was the first time he'd heard that note of depression in her voice. He'd seen her angry, ready to take on him or anyone else if she needed to, but never depressed. Tess was a fighter, but this meeting must have really gotten to her.

He turned out the lights and locked up the office. On the way to her house, he watched the rearview mirror, but if anyone was following him, they were too subtle at it to get caught. Neil pulled in between the decorative iron gates, got out of the car, and walked toward the house, climbing the steps to the front porch.

The dim glow of the streetlight barely illuminated the doorway. He paused, feeling eyes were watching him. Instead of ringing the doorbell, he turned to inspect the street. Light glinted off metal. He dropped to the porch floor. A shot rang out, splitting the silence of the night. Neil rolled over into the shadows, half hidden behind a post.

He lay still, listening for the sound of footsteps, hoping Tess wouldn't turn on the light, or worse, open the door. His gun was in the glove compartment of his car. Lot of good it did him there. If he got out of this alive, he was going to carry the thing with him everywhere he went. This was the second time he'd been shot at, and it was getting old.

Nothing moved, except the branches of the large oak, rustling in the wind. Time passed slowly. After what seemed like forever, he heard a car motor start.

He waited a few seconds longer, then got to his feet and pressed the doorbell. A fresh scar marked where a sliver of wood had been ripped from the doorframe. The bullet had come that close to him.

CHAPTER ELEVEN

Neil leaned on the doorbell. "Come on, Tess! Get a move on!"

He glanced over his shoulder, halfway expecting to hear another gunshot aimed at his unprotected back. The porch light flashed on, and he cringed. That made him a target for sure. When Tess answered, he jerked open the storm door and stepped inside, pushing her back into the foyer. He shoved the door closed and put his arm around her, hustling her toward the living room. The television set blared in the background.

Tess pulled back and stared at him. "What's wrong with you?"

"Someone shot at me."

"Was that what I heard? I could hear it even over the television."

"Yeah. They shot at me right out there on your front porch. Almost got me, too."

He hurried to the window and yanked the curtains closed. "Stay away from the windows. I'm going to call the police."

She glanced at the windows and then back at him. "They shot at you?"

"That's right." Neil speed-dialed the number of the police station.

He talked to them more than he called his own mother. The phone rang once, twice, three times. What was this? Were they all out on break?

"Cedar City Police."

"Yeah. Who's this?"

"Burke Palmer. Who were you calling?"

"You." Neil paused to collect his thoughts.

"So, who are you, and what's the problem?" Burke demanded.

"Uh—sorry. It's Neil Vaughn. I'm at Tess's house. Someone took a shot at me, right out there on her front porch."

"Hit you?" Burke asked.

"No, but they tried hard enough. You want to come over and do your investigating thing?" He made an effort to calm himself. It wouldn't do any good to mouth off at Burke; none of this was his fault.

"Yeah, I'm on my way. You know, this used to be a peaceful town until you moved here."

"Right. I'll be waiting for you. Do you want the porch light on?"— the light that threw the entire porch in relief and made anyone standing out there a perfect target. Neil was lucky it had been off when he arrived. Otherwise, he might not be here to tell about it.

"No, leave it off for now."

Neil hung up the phone, and went to the foyer to wait for the police. Tess followed him, her complexion several shades lighter than normal. She reached out to touch him, as if reassuring herself he was really there. He forced a smile for her, hoping to ease her fears.

She was too smart to be fooled. "Were they waiting for you, or did they follow you here?"

He thought about that. "I guess they followed me. They couldn't have known where I was going." He hadn't seen anyone, but it was dark, and while he had seen headlights several times, there was no way of telling if it was just normal traffic or someone trailing him.

A police car pulled into the driveway, and Neil opened the door, watching as Burke and Stanley walked toward him. He stepped out on the porch, ignoring the itching between his shoulder blades. The men climbed the steps and stopped in front of him.

"Okay, what happened?" Burke asked.

Neil pointed to the bullet scar. "I was standing right here. Had a feeling I was being watched. You know how it is. You just know someone is there, even if you can't see them."

"Yeah, I've felt that way a few times," Stanley said. "So what happened next?"

"I looked over my shoulder, saw light glinting off metal, and I dropped, just as they shot. That's where the bullet hit." Looking at the raw scar, he realized what a near miss it had been. Whoever fired that shot meant for it to be fatal.

Tess stepped out on the porch, and he moved to stand in front of her, shielding her from the street. He didn't think the sniper was still out there, but there was no way he would take a chance with her life. She stared up at him, and he had a feeling she understood what he was doing. Burke turned on the porch light, Stanley took a picture of the bullet scar, and then they all went in the house to sit around the kitchen table. Tess pulled the curtains, blocking the view from outside, but Neil knew if anyone decided to shoot through the window, he'd probably hit one of them. After all, they were sitting around the table with nothing between them and the outside but a pane of glass and a flimsy curtain.

He told Burke and Stanley all he knew, which wasn't very much, and they left. Tess looked at him, her lips trembling. "You could have been killed out there."

"But I wasn't." He pulled her to her feet, drawing her close, marveling at the way she fit in his arms. Holding her seemed so right, so natural. She rested her head on his chest, and it was like a shot of energy to his heart. They stood that way for a moment, not speaking, and then she stirred and looked up at him.

"I'm scared. Why are these people trying to kill you? It's not like you have anything to do with my family. I think it's dangerous for you to be seen with me."

He cupped her chin in his hand. "You hush that kind of talk. We're going to find these creeps and put an end to their tricks. And I'm not going to stop seeing you. We're in this together, and that's the way it is."

He gazed down at her, seeing the sweet curve of her smile, the worry in her eyes. He lowered his head, and his lips met hers. The world stood still. He was aware only of the woman in his arms. Gradually he came to his senses and raised his head, searching for the right words to say. She stared up at him, mouth slightly open, and he knew he couldn't let this happen again. As much as he wanted to be with her, he couldn't allow himself to be sidetracked. He had to stay focused. One little misstep could be fatal for one or both of them.

"I'm sorry. That shouldn't have happened."

She moved back, out of his arms, her expression closed. "Will you be safe going home?"

"Probably. I doubt if they'd try again tonight." He sighed, knowing that he'd made a mess of things. She had taken that the wrong way, and he didn't know what to do about it. "I guess I'd better be going. Be sure to lock up after me and set the alarm."

"I will." She followed him to the door and he heard the click of the lock behind him. He walked to his car, halfway expecting to see the flash of gunfire. Nothing happened, but he had a feeling someone was out there watching, just waiting for him to make one little mistake.

He was restless when he reached home. Unable to settle down, and tired of fighting the memories buzzing around in his head, he got out Rebecca's file and thumbed through it. That gunshot on Tess's porch tonight had jarred him. Not just because it had been aimed at him—that was bad enough—but it brought back Rebecca's death all too vividly. She had been shot. In her own home.

What if they had killed him? Would they have gone after Tess too?

Neil didn't need to read the file. He'd gone over it so many times he'd practically memorized it. He stopped at one page, reading the names of the men who had killed Rebecca. Harry Simmons. Lester Holt. Simmons was New York born, but Holt came from Missouri. Or maybe Arkansas. That hadn't been important at the time. Neil had been too overwhelmed at losing Rebecca.

Now he'd met Tess, and her life was on the line. It was like living through the same nightmare. He took a deep breath. *Help me, God. I can't lose this time.*

• • •

Tess dressed casually for her meeting with Erin, as she preferred to be called. That bothered her, as if Rhona had turned her back on her real family. Maybe, with the two of them meeting today, they could form some kind of bond. She pulled on jeans and a lavender T-shirt, and combed her hair back into a ponytail. Probably she should take more pains with her appearance, but she was still upset over last night. She'd work this morning, then take an early lunch to meet with her supposed sister. The events of last night were still tying her nerves in knots.

Neil could have been killed out there. Right on her front porch. She tried to steer her mind away from what happened after Burke and Stanley had gone back to the station. His kiss had left her breathless, wanting more, but he had pulled away, made it clear he didn't intend for it to happen again. Well, she'd see that it didn't. She didn't have to force herself on anyone. She could get by without Neil Vaughn.

Even as she thought it, she knew better. Somehow he had worked his way into her life, taken control of her heart. She looked in the mirror, slapping on makeup. Suddenly she stopped and brought up her hands to cover her face, praying for guidance. She felt like she was surrounded by enemies. Not Neil, of course. Even if he didn't want to get personally involved with her, he would stay to the end, trying to keep her alive. But there were people who wanted her dead, and she didn't know who they were, had no way to protect herself. Only God could help her now. Finally she raised her head, and went downstairs, ready to leave for work.

Most of the employees were just arriving as she got there. Usually she was early, preferring to get settled at her desk before this, but recent events had thrown her off course. It was hard to concentrate on business when someone kept trying to kill her. And now someone had shot at Neil.

The large square concrete building had always been her refuge, her second home. Here she could put away for a little while the feelings of guilt and shame she had carried for so long. Here she could forget that she had been the only one to come home, while losing herself in learning the trade.

Now she took the elevator to her second story office. The sound of machines being started, the flurry of another workday was reassuring, as if her world was getting back to normal, although she knew better.

She was at her desk, looking over her schedule for the day, when Martha came in, bringing her a cup of coffee. Tess smiled. "Good morning. I see Oakland Furniture in Fayetteville called. Is there a problem?"

"No. It seems the sales rep told the store manager about the new line we're developing, and he wants to be first to sample it."

Tess grinned. "That's good. I think it should go well."

"So do I. In fact, I want one of those walnut piecrust tables. I've got a spot in my living room that would be perfect for it." The phone rang, and she hurried to answer.

Tess booted her computer and took a sip of coffee. This meeting today with Erin had her on edge. That and Neil being shot at were all she could think about. Somehow she and Erin had to find common ground, something that would prove beyond all doubt she was Rhona.

At twenty after eleven, Tess pulled into the parking lot of the Country Kitchen, battling another attack of nerves. She'd dreamed of seeing her sister again, but she had always pictured it as a time of joy. They would embrace each other, immediately recognizing that this was a beloved sister. She should have considered that all those lost years would create a gulf between them. She only hoped they could build a bridge.

Tess chose a seat in Maxine's section and waited. Erin arrived wearing tight black jeans, high-heeled black boots, and a green silk shirt. A three-strand necklace of green, blue, and lavender glass beads added glitter and glitz. Tess felt downright dowdy in comparison.

Erin sat down across from her and smiled. "This was a good idea. Just the two of us spending time together."

Tess relaxed a bit. Maybe it would be all right. If they could just sit and talk, they might discover some shared memories. Penny Mason approached their table, carrying menus and glasses of water. Tess looked around for Maxine, seeing her waiting on an elderly couple on the other side of the room. She started to ask Penny why Maxine wasn't working this side of the restaurant, but decided to keep quiet. She didn't want to make Penny think she didn't want her waiting on them.

After they ordered, Erin rested her arms on the table. "I suppose you have a lot of questions, and so do I. Let's get started. You're probably curious about me."

Tess nodded. "Yes. Where have you been all these years? We tried to find you, but every way we turned, we hit a blank wall."

"Probably because that's the way Aggie wanted it. She's good at getting her way."

"But why did she keep you? They took the ransom money for you, but then they never let you come home. They stole the money."

Erin's eyes flashed in sudden anger. "Morris and Aggie didn't steal anything. They wanted me when my real parents didn't."

"That's not true! I grew up in that house. I saw what losing you did to them. They never got over it. If those people told you we didn't want you, they lied."

Tess hacked off a piece of grilled pork chop and bit into it, trying to stem the flow of words crowding her mind. Did this—Erin—know about the will, the last act of a grieving mother who never recovered from losing a child? Was that why she had turned up now?

"Aggie didn't lie," Erin snapped. "She was always there for me, and I'll not listen to your running her down."

Tess placed her fork on her plate and leaned back against the seat. "Why did you come back now? After all these years of hearing nothing, why now? And why aren't you using your real name?"

And why was she acting as if this woman really was Rhona? Tess had questions, but no answers. Before she accepted Erin as her long lost sister, she needed proof. Frank Walpin had supposedly checked her out. She needed to bring more pressure on him, make him show her what he'd learned that made him think this woman was Rhona. He'd kept her in the dark long enough.

Erin made an obvious effort to gain some control over her emotions. "Look, I realize we're approaching this from different directions. We were both children. Our memories are bound to be different. Let's start over, okay?"

"I guess so," Tess muttered, still irked at some of the things Erin had said.

"All right, I'll start with the name. Erin is the name Aggie gave me. I've been Erin for so long, it seems unreal to answer to any other name."

So they took her name, took her identity, made her over into someone else. Tess could see why she had accepted the change. Grown men could be brainwashed. It wouldn't be all that hard to play with a child's mind. She needed to back off and just listen. Maybe she would hear something that would help her learn the truth.

"So where did you go to school?"

"I was home-schooled. Aggie taught me."

"Did you go to college?"

"No," Erin shook her head. "I never wanted to go. All I wanted to do was get a job and start earning money."

"Where do you work?" What Tess wanted to know was what town, what state, something definite. Just one little fact they could follow up on.

Erin shrugged. "I've worked in several places, but enough about me. Tell me something about you. What do you do?"

Tess chewed a bite of salad before answering. Enough about her? So far there hadn't been any real information forthcoming about Erin, just odd bits that didn't seem to fit anywhere. "I've never lived anyplace except in Cedar City. I took care of my parents in the last years of their lives, ran the business, and tried to find you. That about covers it."

"No serious relationships? What about this Neil who was at your house the day we met? Who's he?"

Tess shook her head. "I've not had much time for romance. Neil is just a friend who was there because I asked him to come." She eyed the woman sitting across the table from her. She was pretty, fashion- able, assured, but was she Rhona?

Erin smiled. "You're still not sure about me, are you?"

"I want to be, but I've dreamed of finding you for years. I sort of had a picture of what it would be like."

Erin's eyes sparkled with amusement. "And it's not the way you planned, is it?"

"No, I'm afraid it isn't, but then I suppose I had some unrealistic ideas about it."

"Give it time, Tess. We've got a lot of catching up to do. Life changed for both of us, and it will take a while to put it all together again." She glanced at her watch. "I'm sorry, but I have to go. I've enjoyed just the two of us sitting down and talking. We need to do more of it."

"Yes, we need to spend time together. I suppose it will get easier as we go along."

"Count on it." Erin picked up both checks. "Lunch is on me."

When Tess protested, she grinned. "You can get the next one."

Tess watched her leave the restaurant, and was getting ready to get up and go when she saw Neil enter.

He slid into the booth across from her. "Well, how did it go?"

"I don't know. Part of me wants to accept her, and part of me is holding back. I wish there was some way to know for sure."

"There is."

She glanced at him, inquiringly, and he said, "DNA. That will show if you are related."

Tess nodded. "I mentioned that to Frank, but he hasn't brought it up again. I need to press him a little. He's not very cooperative. Do you think she'd agree?"

"She won't have a choice, if you insist on it."

"No, probably not. Have you learned anything about who shot at you?"

"Not yet. They're still out there, probably waiting for the chance to try again."

Tess suppressed a shudder. Someone was determined to kill them, and there didn't seem to be anything they could do about it.

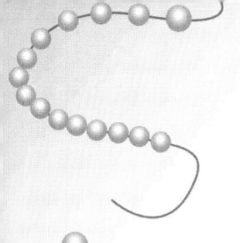

CHAPTER TWELVE

Tess had just finished cleaning the kitchen after breakfast when the phone rang. She let the answering machine take it, the way she'd been doing lately in case it was another of those horrible calls featuring recordings of Rhona's desperate pleas. Frank Walpin's voice came over the line, and she hurried to grab the phone.

"I'm here, Frank. Sorry about that."

"Tess? How are you this morning?"

All right, at least he wasn't angry, so what was the reason for this early morning call? "I'm fine. What's going on with you?"

There was a silence, as if he hadn't expected her to get down to business so quickly. "I just wanted to know how you feel about Erin now that you've met her."

"I don't know her very well yet, and there are still a lot of questions, like where has she been all these years. She never fully answers when I ask." And while Tess was ready to admit that Erin could be her sister, she needed to be sure. It would be horrible if she accepted her and then the real Rhona showed up later. Tess had to walk carefully here. This wasn't the time to rush into anything.

"All of those questions can be answered when she trusts you enough to give you personal information."

"Trust me? Would you like to explain that? You both know who I am. I don't have to prove anything. She's the outsider, and she needs to come up with some details if she wants to be taken seriously."

Why was he pushing Erin at her? So far he hadn't offered any proof either and he was supposed to have checked her out.

"I expect she's had a hard life. She's probably learned not to trust everyone. She might be afraid that, if she bares her heart to you, it could be used against her."

"In what way? Are you saying she's done something illegal? If so, you need to tell me."

Tess hadn't learned how much this work he was doing on her behalf would cost her, but she was sure it wouldn't be for free. It was time to push to see his proof that Erin Clark was really Rhona Howard.

"No, of course she hasn't done anything illegal. What a thing to say," he scolded. "You shouldn't take that attitude. After all the time you've spent trying to find her, it looks like you'd be a little more accepting now that she's shown up."

"I'll tell you what, Frank. You show me your file on her, let me see for myself what you've found out, and then I'll make up my mind. And are you planning to follow through on my suggestion about DNA?"

"Are you saying you doubt my professionalism? Have I ever misled you? I've helped you every way I could, especially since your parents died and you had the burden of running the business by yourself."

Most of his so-called help wasn't necessary in the first place, and running the business wasn't that much of a burden, but this wasn't the time to tell him so. Tess still needed to learn what he knew about Erin, and she couldn't understand why he didn't want to tell her. He was something of a glory hog, she had always known that. Everyone in town knew about the Howard girls' kidnapping. The story had made national headlines. Probably Frank saw this as a way to show the world how wonderful he was. She missed Herbert Davis and his common sense way of looking at everything.

"I appreciate all you've done"—and may God forgive her for that deception— "but this is a delicate personal matter, and I need to know what you've found out about her. I have to be sure, Frank. Like you said, this is too important to leave anything up to chance." There. Let him answer that. She noticed he didn't answer her about DNA. So had he considered it or not?

There was a silence, then he said, "Of course, Tess. Let me get the documents in order, and I'll go over them with you."

"And with Neil Vaughn. I want him to look at the papers, too." She thought he would protest, but after a silence he agreed, although she could hear the reluctance in his voice.

"All right, if that's the way you want it, but you need to be thinking of how to acknowledge Erin. After all, this was a very important case when it happened. You need to let the world know she's returned."

"With television cameras rolling?" she asked drily.

"Of course," Frank replied. "She's come home. She deserves recognition for that. The case needs to come to a satisfying ending."

"I suppose so, but not until I'm sure she really is my sister. You'll get back to me?"

"As soon as I can."

"I'll be waiting."

He hung up, and she sat staring at nothing in particular. She should have pushed him on the DNA, but that would wait for later. Tess knew it would be easy to fool her into accepting false information. That was why she wanted Neil to be there to go over Frank's file. His work as a policeman and as a private investigator gave him the experience she didn't have. She wanted to believe Erin was her sister, but she had to be sure. Doubly sure if Rhona was going to be welcomed home in front of television cameras with Frank Walpin standing there, taking credit for the rescue.

• • •

Neil was busy at his desk, closing out a couple of files and doing billing, when the door opened. Bob came in and sat down. He didn't seem as jovial as usual. In fact, Bob looked downright unhappy.

"What's eating you?"

"You know I've been seeing Maxine at the restaurant."

Had she dumped him? "Yeah, I know that, why?"

"I've been in this business for some time now. You get to where you can recognize when someone is avoiding telling the truth."

"Yeah, most of the time. I've been fooled once or twice, though."

So where was Bob going with this? From the way he was acting, it must be serious. But what could Maxine have to hide? To tell the truth, Neil liked the woman. She was friendly, and Tess had taken to her from the beginning. Not that either fact was a good enough reason to trust a stranger.

Bob cleared his throat. "Well, I've been spending time with her, and I have a hunch she's hiding something."

"Like what?"

Usually Bob was open and talkative about everything. Now getting information out of him was work, the way he strung it out one piece at a time.

"I don't know, but she's awfully interested in Tess."

Neil felt like he'd had the air knocked out of him. "In what way?"

"In every way. She wants to know personal stuff, like what she's done all the years since her sister disappeared. What she thinks about Erin, stuff like that."

Neil thought about it. "I guess that's not all that surprising. It was big news when the girls were taken. She might have heard something about it and be curious, and she hears a lot of gossip in the restaurant. Maybe that's all it amounts to."

Bob looked uncertain. "Maybe so, but I've got a feeling she's hiding something, and she won't confide in me."

"She doesn't know you all that well yet," Neil pointed out, but he was getting a little curious himself. It wouldn't hurt to keep an eye on Maxine, and he had just the man for the job. "You keep on seeing her, maybe she'll let something slip and you'll catch it."

Bob sighed. "Look, I like the woman. Maybe more than like her. I don't want to set up a trap for her."

Neil looked at him in surprise. Bob played the field, never settling down to any one female. This was the first time he'd ever heard him say anything like this. "You're kidding, right?"

"What? You think I can't stick with just one woman?"

"It's not that, but you've never shown any inclination to so far."

"Neither have you, but anyone can see you're half silly over Tess." Bob watched him, a grin lurking in the corners of his mouth.

Neil stared at him, not sure what to say. Had he been that obvious? "Are you telling me to mind my own business?"

"No. Just saying that maybe we're both in the same boat. I'll try to find out what she's holding back, but if it doesn't have anything to do with Tess, then I'll decide whether to discuss it with you or anyone else. I'm not going to hurt her unless I have a very good reason."

"Fair enough."

Bob got up and left, closing the door behind him.

Neil thought about what Bob had said. Was Maxine just acting out of natural curiosity, or was she involved in what was happening? Had she been planted in the restaurant to spy on Tess and report back to whoever was trying to kill her? The thought made his blood run cold. He just might do some checking on Maxine Crowley, himself. Bob didn't have to know about it.

He reached for the phone, wanting to talk to Tess.

● ● ●

Tess was just walking in the door from work when the phone rang. She answered to find Neil on the other end of the line. "I was just thinking about you."

"Something good, I hope," he replied.

"Actually, I wanted to ask a favor. I told Frank Walpin that I wanted to see the information he'd gathered on Erin. He refused at first, then said he had to put it in order. I would like for you to be there."

"No problem. Just tell me when and where. Now I've got something to ask you. I'm going to drive out to Stanley's today—how about riding along with me? You'd get to spend time with me, and see Rattler the Watchdog."

She laughed. "How can I resist an invitation like that?" She needed to get away, just relax and be normal for a while. "Should I meet you at the office?"

"I'll come by there. Say in half an hour. Will that work?"

If she hurried. She'd need to change clothes, check her makeup. She'd have to rush. "Sure, that will be fine."

Tess hung up the phone and ran to her bedroom, pulling clothes out of her closet and tossing them on the bed—her new black jeans, a turquoise knit top. She yanked off the oversized white shirt she wore and headed for the bathroom, giving as much time as possible to her hair and makeup.

It wasn't that she was taking special pains just for Neil.

She stopped and looked at herself in the mirror. Who did she think she was fooling? Of course she wanted to look nice for him. All her life she'd wanted things she couldn't have. Nothing had changed. She was still chasing rainbows.

When Neil pulled into the drive, she was sitting in the porch swing, waiting for him. It had been close, but she'd made it with a couple of minutes to spare. She ran down the steps and got in the car.

As soon as she was buckled in, he started the motor. "I called Stanley before I left, but he didn't answer. Burke said this was his day off, and he planned to work around the farm."

"So what do we do if he's not there?" Tess asked.

Not that she minded riding along, whether Stanley was home or not. It was a relief to get away from her problems and just relax. At least with Neil she didn't have to be watching over her shoulder to see if anyone or anything was closing in on her. She felt safe with him.

Tess slid a glance in his direction, taking in the dark hair curling over his forehead, the relaxed way his hands rested on the steering wheel, the muscular way he filled out his navy blue T-shirt. He looked over at her and smiled, and the golden rays of the sun suddenly seemed brighter. She thought of all he'd done, the many little things that made all of this easier for her. If only they had met normally, like ordinary people, instead of being pitched headlong into this impossible mix of good and evil.

They passed a persimmon grove, the round, orange fruit decorating the branches like ornaments. After a hard frost, the persimmons would start to fall, and they'd be sweeter then. Until the fruity globes were nipped by a freeze, they were sour and puckery. Sumac and sassafras were starting to show fall colors, and acorns from the oak trees littered the road. Tess loved fall, except it brought a sadness with it. Soon the brilliant leaves would tumble down, the purple asters and goldenrod would stop blooming, and winter winds would begin to blow.

Neil grinned at her. "Good to get away for a while, isn't it?"

"Really good. This must be quite a change from New York. Do you like living this far from the big city?" The minute the words left her mouth, she wished she could call them back. He'd left New York because of a personal tragedy. She hadn't intended to bring that up.

He didn't seem to notice though. "I don't miss it a bit. Cedar City is so laid back, I like everyone I've met. For the most part, they've gone out of their way to make me feel at home. And it's just a short jaunt from the city limits to this." He waved a hand toward the countryside. "This sure beats city streets and heavy traffic. I can think better out here."

"I know what you mean. I always feel better when I can get out in the countryside and enjoy God's creation. Do you like being a private investigator?"

He didn't answer for a minute. Finally he shrugged. "Yeah, I like it. I get to use the skills I used in police work, but without all the stress. Here I can set my own pace. I wasn't sure I'd find work in a small town, but it's surprising how much comes along. What about you, Tess? Do you like making furniture?"

"You know, I do. My father loved it, and he taught me everything he could. I guess I never really had a chance to do anything else. He let me start working there while I was still in high school, and it's all I know. Now I can't imagine not doing it."

"You always lived in the same house?"

"For as long as I can remember. I think they bought it right after Rhona was born. Then, when their health failed, I took care of them. So the house and the plant are all I know."

It probably sounded dull to anyone else, but it satisfied her. The only thing missing was Rhona. That had left a blight on their lives. She wondered for a moment what her life would have been like if things had been different. Comfortable and comforting, like her friends' homes had been? No dark cloud hanging over them, none of her mother's sudden tears or her father's silence. No more feeling guilty because she had come home and her sister hadn't.

She felt Neil looking at her, and realized she had stopped talking. "Why are we coming to see Stanley?"

"I've got some questions I want to ask him. He was friends with your father, fishing buddies. They probably did some talking about those phone calls your parents were getting. I don't know if Stan was a cop back then, but I want to dig around in the past and see if we can come up with anything. It might jar your memory too."

Tess thought about what he'd said. "Dad and Stanley were good friends. Maybe he will remember something. And we'll get to see Rattler again."

Neil laughed and turned into the lane to Stanley's house, making the cattle guard clatter, but when they reached the house, Stanley's truck was gone. Rattler got up from lying on the porch and stood on the top step, watching them.

Neil grinned. "Stanley was right. He's a good watchdog."

Tess laughed as he turned around and headed back down the lane. "So what do we do now?"

"How about taking a drive? Maybe take the long way back to town. How does that sound?"

"It sounds great." Funny, she had been feeling depressed, bowed down with her problems, but just being with Neil had cheered her to the point she could put all of that aside and enjoy life for the moment.

When they reached the end of the lane, he pulled out on the main road and turned left. She didn't remember this road. Probably she'd been down it at some time, but if so, she had forgotten.

They'd gone a couple of miles down the road when they passed a large farmhouse badly in need of a paint job. The yard was overgrown, and littered with junk. A couple of cars were parked in the drive. No one was outside.

Neil glanced at the house and then looked back at the road. "Wonder who lives there?"

"I don't know, but I'm not sure I'd want them for neighbors."

Neil leaned over to flip on the radio. Gospel music by a good quartet poured out. He hummed along with the singing. Tess listened with half an ear.

To her knowledge, she had never seen that house before, but something about it made her extremely nervous.

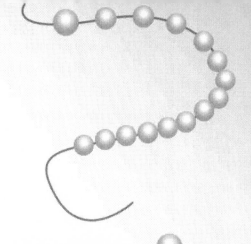

CHAPTER THIRTEEN

Tess stared confusedly at her computer screen, too tired to think straight. She'd gotten behind, and today she'd been playing catch-up—letters she had to answer, forms she had to fill out, things she couldn't delegate to someone else. From the silence surrounding her, everyone had left for home long ago. She glanced at her watch. Ten-thirty. Way past time to leave. Her cell phone rang, and she glanced at it. Neil. What could he want at this time of the night?

She answered, and his voice came over the line, sounding worried. "Where are you?"

Where was she? What was this? Had something else happened? "I'm at the office."

"What are you doing there this late?" Tension crackled in his voice.

She took a deep breath and slowly exhaled. "I'm trying to catch up on work. I've gotten behind lately."

"But you're by yourself? You stay right there. I'm on my way over, and I'll follow you home."

Tess sighed and stared at the opposite wall. Yes, she knew about the danger, but she couldn't go into hiding just because some evil person was after her. She had to trust God and carry on.

"You don't have to do that. I'm about ready to leave, and I'll be just fine."

"I'm on my way, and you stay right there. That's not negotiable." He ended the call, leaving Tess a little bit ticked off.

Yes, he was trying to protect her and she was grateful, but she was exhausted, overwhelmed by trying to run this business, trying to decide if Erin was really her sister, and just trying to stay alive. It was good of him to check on her, but right now she just wanted everyone to leave her alone. She'd be in a better mood tomorrow.

Tess clicked her way through the site, ready to close down. Ten minutes later, she picked up her purse, shut off the lights, and locked the front door behind her. She'd wait in the car until Neil got here. The pole lights in the front parking lot were bright, illuminating the empty expanse that was filled with cars during working hours. The lot at the back, where the trucks parked closer to the loading dock, would probably hold a couple of semis, but the drivers had gone home. She hurried to her car, praying all the way. Although she wasn't about to admit it, Neil was probably right. This could be a bad situation, but it seemed safe enough right now. Tess jerked the door open and crawled inside, feeling more comfortable.

A dark green car drove into the lot, lights off. It pulled alongside of her, and she pushed the button, locking her doors. Two men in dark clothing and ski masks jumped out of their vehicle and rushed toward her. Tess fumbled in her purse for the car keys. The men jerked on the doors, trying to get in.

The car rocked back and forth, slinging her from side to side. The man on the driver's side pounded on the glass. He pressed his face against the window, trying to peer in. The knitted, dark blue mask with white circles around the eyes, and a malevolent red grin twisting the mouth, looked like something out of a horror film.

Tess shoved the key into the ignition and started the motor. Frantic, she grabbed the gearshift, throwing it into reverse. The car shot backwards, knocking down the man standing by the driver's side door. The second man ran after her, swinging what looked like a metal bar. She heard them shouting curses at her.

A black SUV roared into the lot, horn blaring. The two men ran to their car and jumped in. Motor racing and tires spinning, they surged toward the road, lights still off.

She rammed the gearshift into park and got out. Neil rushed toward her and she stumbled into his arms, her pulse racing. He held her, breathing soft words of comfort, until she calmed down. She took one long, sighing breath, and looked up at him, tall, strong, protective. Their gaze locked, and her heart leaped at the concern she saw reflected there. He held her away from him, eyes searching hers. "Are you all right?"

"I am now. You rescued me again." Her voice trembled, in spite of her efforts to keep it steady.

"That's what I'm here for." Neil smiled, but he still looked worried. He glanced around the lot. "Let's get out of here. I'll follow you home."

A shiver of fear snaked through her as she thought of the suddenness of the brutal attack, and what could have happened if he hadn't arrived when he did. Tess breathed a prayer of thanksgiving for Neil Vaughn, and then she put the car in gear and drove home.

● ● ●

Neil watched as Tess pulled out of the lot. He'd arrived just in time. His blood still burned hot with anger. Probably a good thing he hadn't got his hands on those two. He might be facing a murder charge right now. Only cowards would attack a woman that way. Evil cowards.

He turned his car, falling in behind her, trying to keep an eye out for anything irregular. Nothing happened, but he was glad to turn in through the wrought iron gates at the end of her driveway. He got out of the car and walked toward her, and his stomach clenched as he realized how close he had come to losing her.

She pointed at the window on the driver's side, a jagged crack streaking across it. "They were determined to get to me."

He felt a chill, thinking about what could have happened. Thank God he had called her and found out where she was. If she'd been in that empty parking lot alone, she would have been at their mercy. He stepped closer to examine the glass. When he straightened, Tess was watching.

"What do we do now?" she asked, looking close to tears.

"We need to call Burke again."

She made a face. "Do we have to?"

"What do you have against Burke?"

Her eyes widened as she gave him a startled glance. "Nothing, of course. I like him, but it's just that every time I turn around, I'm calling the police. He has to be as tired of it as I am."

"Burke's just doing his job, and he's good at it. Let's go in the house and give him a call."

He followed her to the front porch, glancing around the shadowed yard. Her big, old-fashioned house was beautiful, like her, with a classy elegance not found in modern houses, but it was too isolated. The large yard that offered privacy also hid her from her neighbors. It would be too easy for someone to hide until she let down her guard. She needed better outside lighting, but no doubt she'd protest if he tried to suggest it.

Inside the house, he made sure the door was locked behind them, and then he made a tour of the downstairs rooms before speed-dialing Burke and giving him a short summary of what had happened.

There was a stunned silence. "Man! They're really after her, aren't they? Did you get a good look at them?"

Neil stopped to think. "They wore black pants and shirts, and ski masks. They were driving a late-model dark green Ford. Other than that, I can't think of anything that would identify them. It happened so fast, and I was trying to get to Tess before they got their hands on her. I didn't even think about getting the license number."

"Okay. We're on our way. Stay inside until we get there."

Neil hung up the phone and turned to Tess. Anger burned through him again as he thought of her helpless, scared, those brutes trying to break into her car. He reached for her, pulling her close, and she leaned against him as if seeking shelter. He rested his chin on top of her head, feeling the silken strands of her hair brush against his face.

The wall clock in the living room chimed eleven. He turned her around and walked in that direction, his arm around her shoulders.

She moved to the Queen Anne chair upholstered in a gold, brown, and rust patterned material. Neil took the recliner while they waited for the police. His gaze lingered on Tess, sitting stiffly, hands clasped in her lap, and he wanted to hold her again, comfort her, but he didn't dare. He had to keep a clear head, concentrate on keeping her safe.

The doorbell rang, and Tess jerked her head around. Neil motioned for her to stay seated. "I'll get it. It's probably Burke."

He strode through the living room to the foyer, seeing the bulk of the policeman filling the other side of the glass in the door. They'd left the porch light on, which could be good or bad, depending on what played out. When Neil opened the door, the concern on Burke's face got to him. The guy really cared about the people it was his job to protect.

Neil stepped aside to let him in, followed by Stanley who hadn't been visible behind the big policeman. "She's in the living room. You know the way."

They headed in that direction, and Neil trailed along behind them.

Burke stopped in front of Tess. "You okay?"

"As well as I can be," she replied, a faint tremor in her voice.

"Right. You hang in there." He stepped around the coffee table and sat on the couch, leaning forward, forearms propped on his thighs.

Stanley patted her shoulder, then took the chair by the door. Neil settled deeper into the recliner, waiting quietly. This was Burke's show; let him ask the questions. Tess leaned her head back against the chair and watched them.

Burke finally spoke, "We looked at your car. In addition to the cracked window, you've got a dent in the passenger door."

She nodded and licked her lips, but she didn't say anything.

Burke waited for a moment before speaking again. From his expression, Neil had an idea he already knew Tess wouldn't be happy about what he had to say. "Look, I went to school with you. We're friends. I don't want anything to happen to you. So no more taking chances. You understand?"

"No, I really don't. So far, these people tried to shoot me in the park, broke into my house, took pictures of me when I didn't know they were anywhere near, and tonight they attacked me at work. I've not been taking chances. I've just been going about my life, and they jump me."

"You worked way too late tonight, with no one else there. That's taking a chance, and you know it. Don't try to tell me you don't."

She pressed her lips together, her expression rebellious. "So what do you suggest? That I go into hibernation? I have a life. I have to shop. I have to get out among people. And it's necessary for me to go to work."

These people were trying to kill her. Didn't she understand that? Neil noticed the tightness of her features, the way she gripped her hands together. Yes, she understood, and she was right. She couldn't go into hiding and still keep up with the factory. Besides, she wasn't all that safe in her own home. Her attitude right now was because she was still scared, not able to calm down yet. From the look on the cops' faces, they realized that too.

Burke nodded, looking sympathetic. "I'm not asking you to do this forever, just until we have time to catch these guys. We'll get them eventually. They'll do something stupid and we'll nab them. But for right now, I want you to stay around people, no more setting yourself up like you did tonight."

"Have you learned anything new in the case?"

"No, but we will. We're giving it top priority. Now how about it? You going to use some common sense and make sure you're not alone out there, and that you leave work at a reasonable hour, or are you going to just go your merry way, leaving us to pick up the pieces?"

She frowned, but before she could say anything, Stanley spoke up. "Look, I know you don't like this, Tess. I wouldn't like it either. But I'm not anxious to attend the funeral of my old friend's daughter. Now, instead of fighting us on this, how about playing along. It wouldn't hurt, and it could save your life."

Tess looked at him before glancing at Neil. He nodded. "I'm with them. Tonight was too close for comfort. If I hadn't showed up when I did, no telling what they would have done. Probably killed you, judging from how determined they were to get you out of that car."

They'd used clubs of some sort, tire tools or something like that. If they'd hit her with one of those blunt instruments, she wouldn't be sitting here in the living room in her own house. She'd be lying in a deserted parking lot, waiting to be discovered. Or maybe they would have taken her away. Either scenario scared him.

The men watched her, and finally she heaved a sigh. "All right. I understand and I appreciate all you're trying to do. I guess I can go along with it for a few days."

She looked a little more relaxed, and even managed a faint grin. Neil nodded. She was a fighter, all right.

"You got it," Burke said, getting to his feet. "Come along, Stan. We've got work to do. You staying for a while, Neil?"

"Thought I would, unless Tess has other plans."

She frowned at him. "What plans could I have? It's the middle of the night. You might as well go on home."

He grinned, and shook his head. "I will, after I make sure you're okay." After he searched this house. He'd see that she had the alarm turned on, too. She was probably nervous about staying here alone, but she wouldn't admit it. This was one stubborn woman. And he intended to keep an eye on her whether she liked it or not.

He followed Burke and Stanley to the door, locking it behind them. When he returned to the living room, Tess still looked a little belligerent. "You don't have to babysit me. I'm a grown woman, and I'll be just fine here by myself."

"We don't know that. Isn't there somewhere else you can spend the night? How about calling a friend?" He knew before he asked that she would say no, but he had to try.

She shook her head, lips pressed firmly together. "Wherever I go, they can track me. I'm not about to put someone else in danger."

This house was too big, too empty with just one person staying here. She stared at him, meeting his eyes, and he stifled a groan. All right, she wasn't going anywhere, and there wasn't anything he could do about it. "At least let me search the house to make sure you really are alone."

He got up and led the way to the kitchen. Starting there, they went through every room downstairs then they climbed to the second floor. He'd never been up here before. There were four bedrooms and a full bath. He paused in the doorway of Tess's bedroom, recognizing it because of the lived-in look. The other rooms were sterile, as if no one ever came into them. This one had a book lying on the nightstand, a robe tossed over a chair, and a pair of running shoes lying half under the edge of the four poster bed. A fancy chest of drawers, like the one his mother had, held several pictures. He figured they were family photos. Finally, satisfied that they were alone, he descended the stairs, with Tess following.

In the foyer, she reached out to touch his arm. "I'm sorry I was so irritated. It was just my nerves raging out of control. I've calmed down some now. I appreciate all you've done for me tonight. You saved my life. It's getting to be a habit."

"Glad I could be of service." He placed his hand over hers. "Now, I know you need to get some sleep, so I'll leave. But if anything disturbs you—anything—you call me and I'll be here."

"I will, and Neil, thank you again."

Tess stepped away from him and opened the door. He reluctantly walked out "Be sure to set the alarm."

She nodded, smiling up at him. "I will. That's become an important part of my everyday ritual."

He touched her cheek, rubbing his thumb over the corner of her lips. Then he walked across the porch and down the drive to his car. When he reached it, he turned and looked back, but she had already shut the door.

Neil drove around the block and parked where he could see the upstairs lights in Tess's home. When they went out, he shifted into drive and inched closer, parking in a vacant lot across the street where he had a clear view of the front of her house. Whether she liked it or not, he was keeping watch. He didn't expect the thugs who had attacked her to try again tonight, but he was ready, just in case. He wasn't about to drive off and leave her unprotected.

● ● ●

Worn out from tossing and turning, Tess stared at the ceiling. She couldn't sleep. The memory of the attack was too strong, too close. Her nerves were shot. She'd argued with Burke and Stanley, been irritable with Neil. Been a real pain. Keep on like this and she would push away everyone who was trying to help her. She had to get herself under control.

God, I'm sorry. This has worn me down. I can't think, I just want to run away and never look back. Help me. I need a clear head and calm nerves.

She'd have died out there if Neil hadn't come to her rescue. For some reason, these people were determined to kill her. She had Rose going over the records at Child Search, but without any current information, they were hitting a dead end. Neil and the police were on it, but as far as she could see, there weren't any clues as to who these people could be, no helpful leads or witnesses to point them in a certain direction.

But starting tomorrow, she was going to be more cooperative. Yes, she was frustrated, scared, nerves shot. But with God's help, she would work with the people trying to keep her alive.

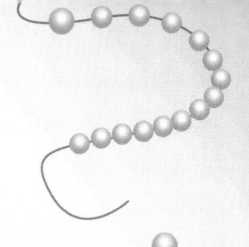

CHAPTER FOURTEEN

Tess spent Saturday morning sitting home alone. She didn't have anything she needed to do, and the events of last night had upset her more than she wanted to admit. After a restless night, she felt extremely vulnerable. If Neil hadn't come, she would be dead now. This was the third time someone had tried to kill her. No wonder she was stressed out, jumping at every sound. She needed something to take her mind off all that had happened lately—maybe one of those mind-numbing sitcoms that passed for entertainment these days.

She was searching for the television remote when the phone rang. She waited for the answering machine to pick up. There hadn't been anymore of those gut-wrenching phone calls, but she didn't feel like taking the chance. Erin's voice came over the line, leaving a message, and Tess grabbed the phone. "I'm here. Just now got to the phone."

"I was getting ready to hang up," Erin said. "Where were you?"

"Just here in the house," Tess said evasively. "What are you up to this morning?"

"How do you feel about getting together again? Maybe today."

Tess hesitated then realized she was being silly. Erin was no threat to her and they needed to spend time together. "Sure, that would be fine. Why don't you come out to the house? No one would bother us here, and we can relax and let down our hair and really talk."

"Sounds good. I'll be there in about twenty minutes. Thanks, Tess. I'm looking forward to this."

Erin ended the call, and Tess closed her eyes, just now remembering what she had promised Neil, and Stanley and Burke. They would see this as going against her word. She should have asked Erin to meet her somewhere more public, but she wasn't going to call back and change things now. Besides, she just realized she didn't have Erin's cell phone number. She'd ask for it today.

Tess hurried to the bathroom to slap on some makeup and run a brush through her hair, pulling it back into a ponytail. Her jeans and denim shirt were fine. Casual dress would set the tone for the meeting, keeping it relaxed and informal—she hoped. The last meeting had been a little tense.

Exactly nineteen minutes later the doorbell rang, and Tess went to answer it. She was relieved to see that Erin was dressed more casually today, too—jeans, running shoes, and a burgundy pullover. Tess looked past her to see a white Buick sitting in the driveway. Erin had nice wheels. Maybe her life hadn't been so bad after all. It would be nice if Tess could stop feeling guilty for all she'd had and Rhona had missed out on. She needed to remember she didn't know anything about how her sister had lived.

"Come on in to the kitchen. I've got a pitcher of tea ready, and there's Coke and Pepsi. What do you prefer?"

"Pepsi, please." Erin settled down in a chair and leaned back. "This is a good idea, just the two of us. Better than having an audience."

"I think so, too," although Neil and Burke would probably have a fit when they found out. Tess felt a little guilty at not telling them, but she couldn't call them every minute and report in. She wasn't used to answering to anyone, and it went against her nature to change, but she knew they were right, and she had promised.

After all that had happened, she needed someone in her corner, and she was grateful to have them watching out for her. After this, she would go along with them, but surely she would be all right meeting the woman who might be her sister in the privacy of her own home.

She filled glasses with ice and brought them to the table, along with the pitcher of tea and a can of Pepsi for Erin, then sat across the table from this woman who was beginning to seem more and more likely to be her sister.

Erin looked around the room as if memorizing the contents. Tess watched, not saying anything.

Erin looked back at Tess, smiled, and shook her head. "You'd think it would be more familiar to me, but I guess it's been too long, and some things have probably been changed."

Tess nodded, feeling sorry for her for the first time. It would be hard to come back after so many years and try to fit in. After all, Rhona—Erin—had been very young. "What do you remember?"

"Not that much. My memories are all about the life I've lived since then. I was only six when I left."

"When you were taken," Tess corrected. She had no intention of whitewashing the horrific crime those people had committed against her family.

Erin shrugged. "That was Aggie. She couldn't have children, and she wanted a child so badly, she refused to give me up."

Tess felt a slow burn of anger. That selfish, evil woman had just taken what she wanted with no thought of what she was doing to the child or to her parents. "So she took my mother's daughter and destroyed our family."

She couldn't keep the bitterness out of her voice. Tess expected Erin to protest, but she just looked solemn, eyes averted.

Erin drew a deep breath, as if what she was planning to say was hard to put into words. "I'm beginning to see what it must have been like. I never thought of what you were going through. I guess I was so focused on myself to the point I ignored everyone else."

Tess looked out the window, blinking back tears, praying for peace, for strength, for wisdom to know the right words to say. "I suppose I'm guilty of that, too. But I lived with the grief and despair we all felt. Nothing was ever the same after we lost you."

And, yes, she was coming around to accepting Erin as her sister. She didn't feel any bond of kinship yet, but that would surely come. She had been living in a fantasy world where she and Rhona had the same feelings, the same emotions, but now she could see that was impossible. They had been ripped apart when they were too young to understand what had happened, and they each had been formed by their experiences since then.

"Are you going to keep calling yourself Erin?"

It would break her heart if her sister rejected the name her parents had given her, or decided not to wear her father's last name. For Tess, her father's name was a badge of honor. Richard Howard had been a decent, God-fearing man, willing to help others. Not like Morris Clark, who left a path of destruction, pain and loss in his wake.

Erin sighed, and shook her head, wearing a reluctant expression. "It will be like giving up my identity, but I guess I'd better get used to being called Rhona. It seems strange to think of myself that way, but I suppose I'll adapt to it in time."

Get used to it? Get used to using the name her parents had given her? It hurt Tess to hear Erin speak so casually like that. But no need to start an argument. She'd done that the last time they got together, and hadn't accomplished one thing. She supposed Erin had loyalty to the people who raised her. She could understand that, but she didn't like it.

Tess smiled sadly. "I'm sure it will all get better in time. We have a lot of catching up to do, and I have a feeling we both have some adjustments to make."

Erin nodded. "I suppose you're right, but I noticed the other day you were referring to our parents as your parents. They were mine, too."

Tess stared at her, appalled. She had realized once she was doing that, and had meant to stop. How could she have been so insensitive? "I'm so sorry, Erin. I just didn't catch what I was doing. I'll try not to do that again." She needed to watch what she said. After all, it was her job to make Erin feel welcome, not drive her away by making her think she didn't belong.

Erin swiped at her eyes. "You don't fully believe I'm your sister, do you? I wish there was some way to prove it."

Here was her chance. Throw it on the table and see how it was accepted. Apparently Frank hadn't brought it up. If not, why? "Actually, there is a definite way to determine if we're related."

Erin stared at her, looking as if she was extremely wary all of a sudden. "There is? What is it?"

Tess took a deep breath, and locked eyes with her. "There's DNA testing. Are you willing to do that? Then we can both be sure you're really Rhona. And a DNA test would silence the gossip from people who live in Cedar City."

Erin slumped in her chair. "DNA? You really don't believe we're related, do you? You know what, Tess? I don't think you want Rhona found. If you did, you'd be a little more accepting."

Not want her found? After all the years she'd given to searching for her missing sister? Tess struggled for the words to say without blasting Erin for her unfeeling remark. "If I really want her found? You have no idea what all I've gone through, what I've done to find her, and you say something like that to me?"

Tess was through being nice. So far, it hadn't done any good.

She didn't have to prove anything. Everyone in town knew Tess Howard. Let Erin prove her own identity.

"Look, I'm sorry," Erin said, "but it's so frustrating. Here I am, finally free to come home, and the one person left of my family doesn't want me."

"Doesn't want you? That's ridiculous. And what do you mean free to come? What kept you from coming years ago?" Tess carefully set down her glass, pushing it to the middle of the table, where it wouldn't be so easy to knock over—or to pick up and throw. She was about three seconds from slipping and telling Erin exactly what she thought, which wouldn't do much for the peace process.

The doorbell rang, and Tess stood to answer it. "I'll be right back."

"Are you expecting company?" Erin demanded. "I thought this was supposed to be just the two of us."

"No, I'm not expecting anyone, but I don't just not answer my door, especially when I'm home and my car is parked out in front."

Tess walked away before Erin could say anything more. She opened the door and found Neil standing there. His coming would probably break up the meeting, and he was about to discover she'd broken her word about not spending time with someone without telling him. She led the way to the kitchen.

Erin shook the ice in her glass, and then drained the last drop of liquid from it. She looked over the rim at Neil, and her eyes widened. "I thought it was supposed to be the two of us. Maybe I should have brought Frank." She set the glass down with a thump and reached for her purse.

"Don't let me run you off," Neil said. "I can leave."

"No, that's all right. I need to be going anyway. I'll talk to you later, Tess." Erin stalked out of the kitchen, and the front door slammed a few seconds later.

Tess turned to Neil. "Sit down. I'm just going to make sure she really left."

She walked out, going to the foyer, not giving him time to protest. He was going to be unhappy with her for being alone here with Erin, but how was she going to get to know people if she didn't talk to them face to face? She'd just let him chew her out and get it over with.

● ● ●

Neil watched as Tess came back to the kitchen. She sat down across from him, a troubled frown on her face. Was she unhappy with Erin or with him? Too early to tell, but from the way she kept glancing at him, she wouldn't leave him in the dark for long.

"I'm sorry I broke up your visit with Erin. What did she want?" He could start out this conversation by giving her a lecture on the dangers of meeting someone without having another person present, but it would just make her angry, and she'd shut him out.

Tess filled a glass with ice and tea, and set it in front of him before answering. "Just to talk. She seemed quieter, not so prone to get upset, until I mentioned DNA. That sort of set her off. She thinks I don't trust her enough to accept her, that I'm trying to disqualify her."

Neil hesitated before deciding to go ahead and ask. "Do you think she's your sister?"

Tess glanced out the window before looking back at him. "Do you think if I acknowledge her as Rhona these attacks against me would stop?"

No. He was afraid they would intensify, especially if the attacks had something to do with the will. He'd talked to people, Bob had talked to people, they'd both searched the Internet, checked with Burke, and neither of them couldn't find anything that could be behind the attempts to kill Tess—except the will.

"That sounds like you think she's behind the attacks," he said, feeling his way. He'd get more out of her if he didn't make her angry.

"No." She paused, looking thoughtful. "I'm not sure what I think. I just know someone is trying very hard to kill me, and I'm afraid one day they'll succeed."

Calm, matter-of-fact, she had just said the words he shrank from speaking to anyone, although they were constantly lurking in the back of his mind. He had tried to lock them away in some mental drawer, but it was no use. He couldn't stop thinking it.

CHAPTER FIFTEEN

On his way home from Tess's house, Neil admitted he was spending a lot of time there. It seemed like he couldn't stay away from her for very long. He never intended to get in this deep. What had started out as just doing a good deed for someone who needed help, and trying to figure out where he fit into the attacks, had accelerated to where he was seeing her face in his dreams. He never expected anything like this, hadn't wanted it, but his feelings for Tess were stronger than his willpower. He wanted to be with her as much as possible—wanted to keep her safe as possible. Somehow she had taken Rebecca's place in his heart. No, not that. She had made her own place. Rebecca had been his first love and she would always remain a part of his life, but any future he had now would be with Tess. At least, he hoped so.

A siren sounded behind him, and he glanced in his rearview mirror. A car, red light flashing, followed close behind. Neil pulled over, wondering what he had done wrong. Something about the car struck him as odd. It wasn't the kind used by the Cedar City police. He reached for his cell phone and dialed Burke.

"Hey, I've got a car here with a red light on the top, but it's not one of yours. You got any undercover cop cars out on the road?"

"We don't have any undercover cars, period. What's happening?"

Neil continued to watch the mirror. "Two guys are getting out and heading my way. They're not in uniform."

"You get out of there. Now. I've got a real cop car on the way."

"Got it."

Neil had left the motor running. Now he shoved the gearshift into drive and tromped the gas. His car shot out onto the road, leaving the two men running after him. He heard the sound of a gunshot before he got out of range. A few minutes later, he heard sirens coming. Maybe they would get there in time to catch the guys. He drove to the police station to make a report, taking extra care to watch for anything that didn't seem right, but nothing more happened.

He knew the police were doing all they could trying to find these guys. He'd been out talking to people too, but no one he'd questioned could tell him anything, and he'd turned up absolutely nothing on the Internet. If they caught these guys, they were going to need God's help.

He noticed he was thinking more about God these days, and praying. It felt good. Yes, he believed God would help them, but in His time, His way. Neil wanted action right now. Waiting on the Lord was all right to talk about, but it could be hard on the one having to do the waiting.

● ● ●

Tess ate breakfast, a bowl of cold cereal and a cup of coffee, and dressed for work. She'd been neglecting business lately. A quick glance at her watch showed she was running late. Grabbing her purse and car keys, she stepped out on the porch, pulling the front door shut and locking it behind her.

She had just started down the steps when she saw sunlight winking off metal. Looking down, she spotted a shiny wire stretched across the second step down. She grabbed for the railing, but it was too late. Her foot caught the wire, throwing her off balance, her purse and keys sailing through the air as she twisted, trying to catch herself. Tess bounced down a couple of steps, landing in a crumpled heap. Pain stabbed through her leg, and she looked down to see a hole torn in her good navy blue pants. Blood seeped through the ragged opening.

She slowly pulled herself up, wincing at the pain. After picking up her purse and keys, she inched her way up by gripping the railing and taking it one step at a time, being careful to avoid the wire. Inside, she headed for the bathroom to bathe the scrape and apply ointment and a large Band-Aid. After pulling on a different pair of pants, she called the police.

Ten minutes later, Burke pulled into the drive. He stopped at the bottom of the steps, looking at the wire before glancing up at her. "You okay?"

"I hurt my knee and ruined a good pair of pants, but other than that, I'm all right."

"Well, you're lucky if that's all you got out of it."

"Burke, are you finding out anything about who's after me?" She couldn't go on like this. Only by the grace of God had she survived this long.

"We've got a few leads, but nothing positive yet. So far they seem to be random, spur of the moment attacks that don't leave much behind in the way of evidence. But we're working on it, Tess, and we're due a break soon."

He bent over and removed the wire, coiling it around his fingers. "I'll take this with me. Where will you be today?"

"I'll be at work all day and here at night. I don't get out much anymore."

He nodded approval. "That's probably good. I'll have someone patrol this neighborhood tonight, and I'll be in touch."

She watched him leave, then locked her front door and gingerly descended the steps. Tess drove to work, favoring her right knee, and put in a full day, not even going out to lunch. A sandwich from the vending machine, and a cup of office coffee strong enough to walk, got her by to closing time.

When she arrived home, she found Maxine Crowley sitting on her front steps. Tess parked the car and got out, wondering what the waitress was doing here, and how Maxine had learned where she lived.

Maxine rose to her feet. "I hope you don't mind me waiting for you like this. I just wanted to talk to you, so I dropped by, and then realized I should have called first. I hope it's all right."

"Have you been waiting long?" Tess stepped past her and unlocked the front door, moving back to let Maxine in. She closed and locked the door behind them before moving from the foyer to the living room.

Maxine stopped, looking around. "You have a lovely home."

"Thank you, I like it. Let's sit down and get comfortable." Tess chose her usual Queen Anne chair, and Maxine sat on the couch. Tess waited. Her knee still hurt, and right now she wasn't feeling too friendly toward anyone.

Maxine took one last glance around the room and then looked back at Tess. "I'm new in town, and working at the restaurant doesn't give me much time for exploring. I'd like to find a church to attend. Nothing fancy, just a simple church that preaches the Bible and makes newcomers welcome. I was wondering where you go. It wouldn't be so hard to walk into a church full of strangers if I knew at least one person."

If Maxine wanted a church, she couldn't be up to anything too bad, could she? "I go to West Avenue Baptist. Neither too small nor too large. I think you'd like it."

Maxine looked puzzled. "I don't know where that is. You'll have to give me directions."

"No problem. I have a brochure about the church, and it has a map in the back. I'll get it for you."

Tess got up and walked into the kitchen. It took her a couple of minutes to find the brochure and take it back to the living room. When she returned, Maxine was standing in front of the fireplace, looking at the pictures on the mantle. She picked up a photograph of Tess's parents, gazing at it intently before putting it back and glancing around the room with a peculiar air of ownership. As if this all belonged to her. Tess rethought their friendship. She didn't know this woman very well, and the attacks had started soon after Maxine came to town. Was she behind the attempts on Tess's life? If so, was Erin safe? If these attacks were linked to the kidnapping, then it wouldn't be enough to kill Tess. They'd have to kill the woman who apparently was Rhona Howard.

Maxine turned and saw her standing in the doorway. She smiled and indicated the pictures on the mantle. "Are these family pictures?"

"Yes," Tess answered stiffly. "That's my parents."

Maxine picked up a group picture. "Is your sister in this one?"

"Yes, right there." Tess pointed out Rhona.

"I hope you get her back." Maxine replaced the picture and reached for the brochure. "I appreciate this, and I'm looking forward to seeing you there."

She glanced around the room one more time, then turned toward the foyer, and Tess followed her to the door, wondering why she had really come. There were several churches in Cedar City, and anyone Maxine asked would be happy to give her directions to one. Something about this visit didn't ring true.

An hour later, Neil dropped by, and Tess was surprised at how glad she was to see him. She invited him in, but decided not to tell him about Maxine, afraid he'd think she was silly for imagining there was something off-key about the visit.

She was jumpy, expecting danger on every corner, but just the same, this thing with Maxine felt strange.

• • •

Neil followed her to the kitchen, accepting a glass of iced tea. "Have you seen Erin again since the other day?"

"No, she hasn't gotten in touch, but Frank wants to hold a news conference and tell the world that Rhona Howard has come home."

"Are you going to do that?"

"I haven't decided yet. I can't prevent him from holding the meeting with the press, but I still want to see his proof that Erin is really my missing sister. I am starting to think she is, but I'd like to see something positive."

"It's going to look strange if they call in the press and you're not there."

"I know. And it would probably drive a wedge between me and Erin. And that's another thing. It's hard for me to fully accept her when I have to call her by another name. When she starts calling herself Rhona, I'll find it easier to acknowledge her."

"Hang in there. Make Frank show you the proof before you agree to anything."

Tess sighed, and then looked at him with such a solemn expression his stomach clenched. What was coming now? He was sure something had happened from the way she was acting, her eyes meeting his, never looking anywhere else. "Okay, you've got something to tell me, let's hear it."

She glanced down at her hands folded in her lap, and then back up at him. "I was going to work this morning—in a hurry, as usual. Someone had fastened a wire across the second step from the top. I tripped over it, and fell down the steps."

Neil's heart kicked into high gear. These people didn't give up. "Were you hurt?"

"It skinned my knee and ruined the pants I was wearing, but that's all. The thing is, who could have done it? If the sun hadn't been shining on it just right, I might not have seen it in time to try to catch myself. It could have been worse."

She could have hit her head on one of the steps, and been lying there dead. He couldn't be with her all the time, but it seemed like the people trying to cut her down knew when she would be alone. Was he just being fanciful, or was someone spying on them? "I'll look at it. Someone had to put it there last night."

Had the men from the parking lot been prowling around here in the dark? His mind reeled at the thought. She'd been lying upstairs, asleep, defenseless, while someone set a trap for her. Tess looked forlorn, like a lost child. His arms reached out, almost on their own, pulling her close against him. He held her tight, feeling her heart beating—or was that his?

She clung to him, and he put one finger under her chin, tilting her head up to look at him. Their lips met, and there was nothing gentle about this kiss. He felt the warmth from it spreading through him, making him forget everything, except the woman in his arms, the woman someone was trying to take away from him.

Tess pulled away, and he could see the confusion in her eyes.

She sighed and put her hands on his shoulders, pushing him away. "I think you'd better go." Her voice was husky, her eyes bright, and he had a feeling she was fighting tears.

Neil took a deep breath and stepped back, knowing she was right. He needed to go before things got out of hand. Leaving her alone was one of the hardest things he'd ever had to do, but it had to be done.

He nodded. "Lock the door behind me, and set the alarm."

She nodded, and followed him to the door. Once outside, he stood for a moment, breathing in the cool air, wondering what waited for him out here.

● ● ●

After dinner, Tess sat in the living room, thinking over the events of the past few days. She had never dreamed she would be under siege like this. All those years of searching for Rhona and nothing happening, and now that she might have found her sister, it was doubtful she'd live long enough to enjoy being together again.

The doorbell rang, and she got up to answer it, flipping on the porch light so she could see who was standing outside. Tess peered through the glass of the door, feeling a chill snaking up her spine. No one was there. She maneuvered around to look sideways through the glass, but couldn't see anything. Something caught her eye, a flicker of movement, a dim figure flitting through the shadows just out of reach of the probing beams of light. Tess stood watching for a long time, but saw nothing more.

Finally, reluctantly, she turned off the porch light, checked the door again, and then turned out all the lights except for one table lamp in the living room. She had never left lights burning at night before, but now she felt safer with one turned on. Maybe anyone lurking outside would think she was still up instead of sleeping helpless in her bed.

A few minutes in the bathroom, brushing her teeth and removing her makeup, and she was ready to put on her pajamas and crawl into bed. Turning out the light brought the darkness closing in on her, like a smothering blanket. After tossing and turning for the better part of half an hour, she crawled out of bed and went to stand by the window.

A sudden gust of wind stirred the branches of the old oak, revealing a figure standing in its shadow, staring up at the window. Tess sucked in her breath. What was Maxine Crowley doing in her yard at this hour of the night?

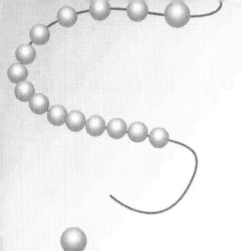

CHAPTER SIXTEEN

Neil had just settled down in front of the television with a cup of coffee when the phone rang. Sergeant Burke Palmer's gruff voice sounded in his ear. "You might want to come down to your office. Looks like someone broke in."

Neil jerked the receiver away from his ear and stared at it, then clamped it back. "Say what?"

"Someone broke into your office tonight. I saw a flashlight flickering around there, and checked it out. When I knocked on the door, whoever was inside ran out the back. I was a little too late getting around there, so I missed them, but they were driving a dark green Ford."

"I'll be right there." Neil dropped the receiver into the cradle and lunged to his feet. What could anyone be looking for in his office? Maybe someone who knew him from New York City nosing around about one of his old cases. Then again, it could be one of the files he was working on, or the thing with the Howard sisters? He was betting on the latter. It seemed everywhere he turned, something new popped up concerning Tess and her sister.

He drove to his office and stopped in front. Burke's patrol car was there, the policeman leaning against it. "About time you got here."

"You been inside yet?"

"No, thought I'd wait for you." Burke straightened and moved out of the way. "Got an APB out on that green car. Haven't found it yet."

Neil unlocked the door and stepped inside, flipping on the lights. Drawers were pulled open, files scattered over the floor. Burke stepped past him, and Neil suppressed the urge to start picking up papers and sorting them into some kind of order. He used to be a cop. He knew better than to disturb evidence, but this was his office, his files.

Burke indicated the computer, sitting over on a table instead of on the computer desk where it belonged. "You keep your computer over there?"

"No." Neil moved toward it. "It looks like they were going to take it with them." It was password-protected, but that probably wouldn't be a barrier to anyone who knew anything about computers.

After looking around the office, he couldn't find anything missing, but he was just giving everything a quick once-over. He'd come back in the morning and do a better job. He doubted very much this was a random crime. The people who broke in had to be looking for something specific.

Half an hour later, he locked the door behind him and headed for his car, watching as Burke pulled out of the lot. He'd put a makeshift lock on the back door, replacing the one the intruders had broken to get in. Tomorrow he'd have an alarm system installed, something he should have done weeks ago. He thought of Tess, and wondered if she was all right, but it was close to midnight. Too late to call her. He'd check in first thing in the morning.

● ● ●

Tess had decided to take the morning off from work, one of the advantages of being the boss, and was sitting at the kitchen table with the files she'd brought home spread out in front of her when the phone rang. She absently reached for it, then remembered she was letting the answering machine screen her calls. Too late now. "Hello?"

"Tess?" Neil's voice came over the line. "You okay?"

"Of course. Why, what's wrong?" What had brought on the anxiety in his voice? Had something new happened? She surely hoped not.

"I'm just checking. Someone broke into my office last night."

"Did they do any damage?"

"None that I can see. I was just afraid they might have paid you a call, too. I'm glad nothing happened."

"No, everything's calm here for a change, but I do have something. Remember I promised you I'd go through the files, looking for the names of the men the police suspected in the kidnapping?"

"Yes, why?"

Tess picked up a piece of paper and held it in front of her. "Well, according to what I've found, their names were Clyde Perkins and Bill Wheeler."

She heard Neil draw a sharp breath. "Wheeler? Is that what you said?"

Tess glanced at the page again. "That's right. Bill Wheeler. Why? Did you know him?"

"Not personally, no, but I'm investigating a missing person case for a Ralph Wheeler who has vanished. Wonder if they're related?"

"I don't know," Tess said, "but according to a newspaper clipping I found in a file marked personal, Bill Wheeler was killed in a car accident the year after Rhona and I were taken."

"I see. Look, I'm sort of tied up right now. Why don't you bring those papers over here, and we can go through them together?"

"Good idea. I'll be there in a few minutes."

She hung up the phone and gathered up the pages, wondering who had broken into Neil's office, and what they were looking for. Was it related to the attacks on her? She didn't know how all of this would turn out, or if she would even survive to see the end of the harassment, but getting to know Neil had been a blessing, and had enriched her life in many ways. A quick look in the bathroom mirror to check hair and makeup, and she was on her way, carefully locking the door behind her.

• • •

Neil looked up as she entered his office. "Come on in. Don't mind the files on the floor. There isn't room on the desk for all of them. I'll soon have them sorted, and then I can put them back where they belong." He picked up another folder, checked it off his list, and added it to a stack by the corner of the file cabinet.

Tess watched him for a minute. "Do you have everything in hard copy?"

He grinned at her tone of voice. "Well, yes, I do. I also have it in the computer, and backed up on a couple of flash drives. I guess I'm overly cautious, but I want plenty of protection."

"So if they took your files, you'd still have the information."

"That's the idea." He cleared off a space on the desk. "Here. You spread out your papers, and I'll whip this mess on the floor into shape and be with you in just a few minutes." He quickly put the files back in alphabetical order, pausing to carefully read the list in his hand. "That's funny. From what I can tell right now, they're all here except the file on Ralph Wheeler."

According to his wife, Ralph Wheeler was missing, but the woman who sent Neil out to the park had known he was looking for Ralph. So what was going on here? He needed to think about this. Instead, he turned to Tess and the papers she had spread out on his desk.

The silver pendant she wore nestled in the hollow of her throat. Matching silver angels dangled from her earlobes, and an errant sunbeam shining through the front window turned her hair into a golden halo. Neil spared a moment to wish he could change the circumstances, start over, meet her in a normal way and have a normal relationship, instead of having to be looking over their shoulders all the time, wondering what would happen next.

She handed him a sheet of paper. "Here are the names of the two men the police suspected of taking us. But, of course, that information is wrong. It was Morris and Aggie Clark who took us and kept us captive until the ransom was paid."

Then they had let her go and kept her sister. From spending time with her and hearing her talk, he knew that being the only one to come home had damaged Tess in ways no one could comprehend. He hoped to bring her some kind of peace, to help her leave the past and move on toward the future. Whether that future could include him, he didn't know, but he was praying God would make a place for him in her life.

Neil reached for the phone. "I'm going to call Hank Branson. He probably knew everyone back then. It seems strange that Bill Wheeler's name would pop up when I'm looking for a Ralph Wheeler, and that's the only file missing so far."

Back when Hank was running a filling station, he probably knew everyone in town. He must have known the Wheelers. It wouldn't hurt to ask.

Tess fumbled with the papers she'd brought with her, looking for a particular item. "There was a fire at the company about then. Ask Hank about that, too."

He nodded, and waited for Hank to pick up the phone. When the elderly man answered, he sounded tired. Neil identified himself, and spent a few seconds in small talk. "Tell you what, Hank, I've got a question. Do you remember a guy named Bill Wheeler? He was fired from Howard's Manufacturing the same time Clyde Perkins was."

"Sure, I remember him. He was in on that stealing, too, just like Clyde. Didn't amount to much, either one of them. Why?"

"Tess and I were going through the old employment records, and his name showed up. There was also a fire at the company right about then. Do you know anything about that?"

"Not much. I tell you what. If you want to know about that fire, you talk to Bert Cayce. He's out at the Shady Oaks Nursing Home. You know where that is, don't you?"

"Out on North Platte Road, right?"

"That's it. Bert was the janitor when that happened. Good man. Can't take care of himself, but his mind is sharper than mine. You talk to him."

"I'll do that, Hank. Thanks a lot." Neil hung up the phone, and told Tess what he'd learned. "You want to drive out to the nursing home and talk to this Bert?"

She nodded, looking thoughtful. "I remember Mr. Cayce. My father thought a lot of him. I'll enjoy seeing him again, and he might be able to tell us something."

He just hoped they would recognize evidence if they managed to stumble onto some pertinent fact. Right now it just seemed like a confused mess. Nothing appeared to fit with anything else. He hoped Burke was having better luck than they were.

Neil followed Tess out to his SUV, and waited until she was buckled in before he started the motor. She looked pensive, and he wondered what she was thinking. Then she turned and gave him a smile, and his pulse rate kicked into overdrive.

Tess shook her head, as if amused at herself. "I'm doing it again. Every time we set out to talk to someone, I start feeling hopeful, as if this time we might really find out something. You'd think I'd learn it isn't going to be that easy."

Neil reached over and placed his hand over hers, resisting the urge to keep it there. He needed a clear head, so it would be better if he kept both hands on the wheel. Just touching her sent his mind into a fog. "We're due a break. Maybe this will be it."

He drove between the imposing rock gateposts of the nursing home, and parked in the visitor lot. Would Bert be as sharp as Hank had promised?

They stopped at the front desk and asked for Bert Cayce. A smiling, brown-haired woman directed them down the hallway to room 213. Neil thanked her, and they walked in that direction. He glanced at Tess, noticing how she held herself erect, lips tightened, and knew she was nervous. For her sake, he hoped they'd learn something new.

They paused at the open door of room 213. A hefty man with a thick thatch of white hair sat in a wheelchair in front of the window, looking out at a bird feeder flocked with blue jays. Company of a sort, he supposed. The man turned to look at them, eyebrows raised in a questioning expression.

Neil held out his hand. "Neil Vaughn, and this is Tess Howard. We'd like to talk to you for a few minutes, if you don't mind."

Bert's expression lightened. "Richard's girl? The one who came home? It's been a long time since I've seen you. Are you doing all right?"

Tess reached out to take his hand. "Well, we're having a few problems. We hoped you might be able to answer some questions for us."

He used his free hand to pat hers. "I'll do anything I can. You just tell old Bert what you need."

Neil let Tess take the lead. Richard Howard must have been a good man, considering the high esteem felt by the people who used to know him. He pulled up the only chair in the room for Tess, and stood back out of the way.

Tess sat down and leaned forward. "I've been going over some old records, and discovered there was a fire at the company about the time we were taken. Do you remember anything about it?"

Bert nodded. "I sure do. I'm the one who found it. I called the fire department, but there was an extinguisher handy, and I had most of it out by the time the firemen got there. Why?"

"Well, some things have come up. It seems like Clyde Perkins has showed up again, and he's giving me a few problems."

Neil admired the way she was understating the case. Probably she didn't want to alarm Bert, but "a few problems" didn't begin to cover what they were struggling against. He realized this woman could be very persuasive when she chose to be. No doubt she was an excellent employer. He could see her working with her employees, trying to be fair. Tess Howard had a lot going for her, and every time he saw her in action, he admired her more and more.

Bert bristled. "What kind of problems?"

Tess hesitated. "He's sort of harassing me. We think it's tied to the kidnapping some way, but we can't find a connection. What about Bill Wheeler? Where does he fit in?"

"Why, he was Clyde Perkins' brother-in-law. Married Clyde's sister Norah. I heard she died a few years back. Had cancer. Bill and Clyde were both involved in stealing from the company. That's what got them fired. I always figured they were the ones who set the fire, getting even with Richard."

Neil spoke up. "The police suspected them of the kidnapping. Why was that?"

"Well, they were both drunks. Couldn't keep their mouths shut. Bragged all over town that they were going to fix Richard Howard. When the girls disappeared, it seemed natural to suspect they had a hand in it. But I believe they'd both left town by then. I still think there was a connection, though. Clyde Perkins was married to Morris Clark's cousin. They were all tied in there together. All in the family, so to speak."

Neil stared at Tess, and he could see the same realization in her eyes. They had their connection. All in the family, indeed. That's how Clyde could get his hands on Morris's identification. It wasn't much, but at least it was a fact, something that could be verified.

Tess and Bert talked for a few minutes longer. When she rose to leave, Bert stared at her wistfully. "You come back and see me. I get a little lonely some days."

Tess leaned over and hugged him. "I will, and that's a promise. Is there anything you'd like me to bring you when I come?"

Bert grinned. "Well, I'm sort of partial to those Lindor Truffles, the milk chocolate ones. You might bring me a bag of those, if it's not too much trouble."

"No trouble at all," Tess assured him. "And the next time, we'll have a good visit, just talking about things and eating chocolate."

"Can't beat that," Bert said. "I'll hold you to it."

As soon as they were in the car, Tess turned to face Neil. "Now we know the connection between the three men."

He took his time responding. "One thing, though. Wonder where Clyde hides out? He has to have somewhere to stay, and he hasn't checked into the motel again, according to Andrea."

"Maybe he has relatives here somewhere. We can ask Burke."

Neil pulled into the office parking lot. "Or Hank Branson. He's been around longer than Burke. He might remember something."

They went inside, and Tess gathered up her papers. "You want to come out to the house tonight, go over these records and decide what to do next?"

"Sounds like a plan." Not that he expected to learn anything, but it would be a chance to spend time with Tess. He couldn't think of a better way to end the day. In the meantime, he was going to see what he could find out about Frank Walpin. From the way he was acting, he didn't seem to want Tess and Erin to get too well acquainted. It was time to find out if he had a personal interest in all of this.

● ● ●

Tess stopped at the grocery store to pick up a few items. Before she could get out of the car, she saw Erin coming with a very full cart. She sat back and watched as the other woman loaded the trunk of her car. Where was Erin staying, and why did she need so many groceries?

Tess followed her to the exit. Erin drove out onto the main road, cutting in front of a funeral procession. Tess fumed as the cars rolled past, blocking her in. By the time the last car had gone by, Erin was out of sight.

She returned to the store, all the while fighting an uneasy feeling that Erin was up to something.

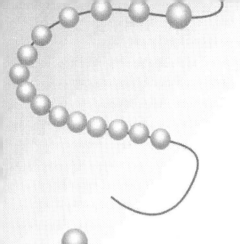

CHAPTER SEVENTEEN

Neil sat staring at his computer screen, not really focusing on the words. Instead he was thinking about Tess. He'd talked to a couple of people about Frank Walpin without learning anything. From what they'd both had to say, Walpin was a local guy, grew up somewhere around here, went away to school and came back home to be a lawyer. After Herbert died, Frank bought out the firm. No one seemed to know anything against him, except he had a high opinion of himself. No law against that. Pass one, and half the population would be behind bars.

The phone rang, and he reached for it. A woman's voice came over the line.

"Mr. Vaughn?"

"Speaking."

"This is Coletta Wheeler, Ralph Wheeler's wife."

"Oh, yes, Mrs. Wheeler"—and he didn't have a thing to tell her.

"I just wanted to let you know that Ralph has come back home. It was all a misunderstanding. We've worked out our differences, and everything is fine."

"I'm glad to hear that, Mrs. Wheeler."

"Send me a bill for what I owe you, and I'll get a check in the mail."

"All right. I'll send it out today."

He leaned back. Something didn't sound right. Ralph Wheeler just came home and everything was fine? No explanation as to where he had been? How did the woman who sent Neil out to the park know he was looking for Ralph Wheeler? Why would someone break into the office, but take only the Wheeler file? There had to be something, somewhere, he was overlooking.

On an impulse, he fished his wallet out of his back pocket and went through it, taking out three pictures of Rebecca and spreading them out on the desk. He had loved her, but she was gone, and he had to move past that time in his life. He'd never forget her, but he was trusting time and God would help him put the memories in their proper place. Rebecca was the past, but why was something about this case reminding him of her? The two cases were nothing alike, but lately he'd found himself thinking of her and of New York City. Maybe it was because another woman he cared about was in danger.

● ● ●

Tess was at her desk, working on payroll, when her secretary told her Frank Walpin was on the line. He got right to the point.

"Tess? I'm setting up a news conference in two days to announce that Rhona Howard has been found."

Her mouth dropped open in surprise. What? "Why are you doing that? After all, I haven't fully accepted her as my sister yet. I want to see some proof she's who she claims to be."

She could hear the bristling anger in his voice. "What is this? I'm your attorney. Don't you trust me?"

"After all I've had to deal with, I don't trust anyone." There, let him take that. If he wanted to continue being her attorney, he could treat her with respect. At this point, she wasn't in the mood to put up with anyone's temper tantrum.

His voice was as cold as a winter day. "I'll present my proof at the news conference. You can be there or not. Your choice."

The line went dead, leaving Tess staring at the wall in frustration. Her hand was still on the receiver when it rang again. She answered to find Neil on the line.

"Hey, Tess, you busy?"

"Not all that much. What's up?"

"I was thinking, you have to eat. I have to eat. How about going to lunch together? I can pick you up in about ten minutes."

Tess thought fast. She should stay at her desk and keep working, but she could take work home—and going to lunch would give her a chance to spend time with Neil, something she was enjoying more every day. "That would be nice. I'll be waiting down in front."

She cleared off her desk, stacking work in neat piles, some to take home, other files to work on this afternoon. When Neil drove into the lot, she was standing outside in the warm fall sunshine, waiting for him. A gentle breeze ruffled her hair, and she lifted her face to the sky, determined to soak up every golden ray. In a few weeks, these comfortable fall days would be a thing of the past as winter moved in.

Neil stopped in front of the building, and Tess climbed into the passenger seat. He turned the car around and headed for the street. "Where do you want to go? The Country Kitchen?"

Something about the way Maxine had been acting made Tess nervous. "No, let's go someplace else."

He shot her a searching glance, but didn't comment. "What about Georgia Ray's Steak House? She puts out good food."

Tess relaxed against the seat, glad he wasn't asking questions she didn't want to answer. After all, she didn't have one ounce of proof that Maxine was up to something. It was strictly her intuition, which probably didn't amount to all that much. "Georgia Ray's sounds good. I haven't been there for a long time."

Inside the restaurant, Neil chose a booth on the far side with no one sitting at the neighboring tables. They ordered from the menu, and then relaxed as the waitress walked away. Neil leaned his arms on the table and started speaking in a low voice. "I got a phone call from Ralph Wheeler's wife. She said I could stop looking for him, because he had come home."

Tess stared at him, thinking furiously. "Where has he been, and why did he just show up again? Did she say?"

Neil shook his head. "No, she didn't explain anything. Just said to send her a bill for what she owed me."

"That sounds strange. What are you going to do now?"

Neil picked up his fork, examining it as if he had never seen one before. "Not much I can do. If she calls me off the case, then I'm off. And she's not going to pay for any work I do after today."

Tess stared at him, eyes narrowed in concentration, daring him to contradict her. "But you're going to keep digging into this, aren't you?"

He gave her a rueful grin. "Am I all that obvious?"

"I'm learning to read your expressions." She was learning to understand him and the way his mind worked. And more important, she was learning to trust him.

They finished eating, and Neil pushed back his plate. "You have time to run by the office? I've something I want to show you."

"Of course." Tess picked up her purse. "Then I have to go back to work. I need to start spending more time on the job. I can't expect it to run by itself. It needs a firm hand on the reins, and since I own it, then it's my responsibility to keep it running smoothly."

• • •

Neil drove Tess to his office, casting glances at her out of the corner of his eye. She seemed to be holding up well, but he had a feeling this constant pressure of never knowing what would happen next was wearing on her. She was tough, but everyone had a limit.

Inside the office, Tess took her usual seat on the visitor side of the desk, and he walked around and dropped into his chair.

She glanced at him, her expression questioning, and he knew he had to come up with something to justify asking her to stop by. "Have you had any phone calls where no one answers?"

"A few. Why?"

"I've been getting them too. I'd guess they're conducting a war of nerves, trying to wear us down."

"If that's what they're trying to do, they're doing a good job. I've stopped answering the phone at home, letting the answering machine pick it up, and I've been screening calls through my secretary. I slipped up when I answered your call, though. I'd just had a call from Frank Walpin that left me so upset I forgot to be careful."

Neil frowned. Frank had upset her? What had he done now? "What's the problem with Frank?"

Tess lifted her shoulders in a shrug. "It's what he's planning to do. He's going to call a news conference in two days to identify Erin as Rhona Howard and tell the world she's come home."

"What do you want to do?"

"I want to see some proof that she's actually Rhona before I accept her. And I want to use DNA, not just accept words on paper. Frank is supposed to be checking her out, but he still refuses to let me see what he's learned. He said he'd present his proof at the news conference."

So Walpin was bypassing Tess. Sure the guy was a glory hog, and he probably wanted his picture on television as the man who had brought Rhona Howard home, but he wasn't being fair to Tess. "Have you decided she's your sister?"

Tess caught her lower lip between her teeth. "I'm leaning that way. I still have some questions though, but I'm not getting any answers."

Neil glanced down at the desk, spotted the pictures of Rebecca, and tried to find something to place over the photographs before Tess noticed them. He was too late. He watched with a sense of impending doom as she reached over and picked them up, holding them spread out in her hand. He wasn't sure what her reaction would be.

• • •

Tess looked at the pictures, examining them one by one. She turned them over and looked at the back. Just as she suspected, they were all of Rebecca. This was a part of Neil's life, and she could understand that, and from things he had let drop, she suspected he was still in love with this woman from his past. So where did that leave her?

She dismissed the thought as soon as it had occurred. They had shared some moments, and she had strong feelings where he was concerned, but right now she had other things on her mind, like this upcoming press conference, sorting through how she felt about Erin, and more important, trying to stay alive. The situation with Neil would work itself out one way or another.

Tess looked at the pictures again. Rebecca had been a lovely woman, with short curly dark hair, a winning smile and perfectly formed features. A woman who would be hard to forget. She placed the pictures back on the desk, and looked at him. "She was beautiful."

He picked up the pictures, and gave them a lingering glance before laying them aside. "Yes, she was."

A silence fell between them, and then he looked at her. "So what are you going to do about this press conference?"

Tess pulled her thoughts away from Rebecca and those pictures. "I don't know. If I take part, then it looks like I believe she's my sister. If she really is Rhona and I refuse to acknowledge her, then I risk driving a wedge between us."

"Sounds like a situation you can't win."

"And I can't force Frank to show me what he's found out. I don't understand why he's behaving like this."

"Well, for one thing, I suspect he wants the credit for solving a high-profile case, and for another, she's a good-looking woman. I hear he has a weakness where they're concerned."

"He also has a wife, though that doesn't seem to slow him down." Tess glanced at her watch. "Right now, it's a mess. I can't stop him from what he plans to do, but either way, it puts me on the spot. Do you need anything? If not, I need to get to work, I'm struggling to keep up, but it's hard to concentrate with everything that's going on."

"I've got to get out and talk to a few people. Maybe I'll get lucky and learn something."

Tess got to her feet. "Then I really have to go."

Neil stood. "Okay, I'll run you back."

They walked out to the parking lot and Tess realized she was reluctant to go back to her office. If she did what she wanted she'd get in her own car and keep driving until she got out of town, out of state—out of reach of the people determined to kill her.

Tess sighed. When had she ever had a chance to just do what she wanted to do? For most of her life, it seemed she'd always had to take care of everyone, fill in at the factory, help her mother, and be a stand-in for the missing daughter. She'd never really had a chance to just be herself.

That was one reason why it was so difficult for her to accept help. She'd always carried a heavy load. Even as a child she'd felt she had to try harder, be more, to make up for being the only one to come home. Then, as she grew older and her father's health failed, she'd had the responsibility of running the business. She'd taken care of her mother until she died. She'd been the one in charge. Now her world had fallen apart. She couldn't control anything. Others were taking over, telling her what to do. It was hard to take. Hard to accept.

Neil pulled up in front of the plant. Tess opened her car door, and he reached over and touched her shoulder. "Stay in touch, okay."

Tess nodded. "I will, and if you learn anything new let me know." She got out of the car and walked back to her office, wishing she could have stayed with Neil. For some reason she felt safe with him. Tess spent most of the afternoon on the phone, trying to track a shipment of upholstery fabric that had gone astray, finally discovering that, due to a glitch in the warehouse computer, her order had never been entered. Paychecks waited for her signature, and her best sales rep was in the hospital with a broken leg. Her life was going from bad to worse. Yes, she was indulging in a pity party, but considering all she was going through, God surely understood.

When she reached her house, Erin was waiting for her. Tess slumped in the car seat. She wasn't up to another confrontation, but it looked like she was in for one, anyway. *God, help me. I don't need another problem to handle right now.* She got out and walked toward the porch, knowing she didn't have a choice. She could either face Erin, or stay in the car and run. She wasn't in a running mood.

Lips drawn into a narrow line, and a frown creasing her forehead, Erin waited until Tess unlocked the door, and then followed her inside. Tess led the way to the living room. When they were seated, she nodded at the woman who claimed to be her sister. "All right, what is it?"

"I want to know why you are rejecting me. I've finally come home, only to find my parents are both dead and my sister refuses to accept me."

Tess looked at her, wondering how much of this rant was sincere. "I'm sorry, but everything has happened so suddenly I feel over-whelmed."

Erin gripped the chair arms and gave her back look for look. "Well, how do you think I feel?"

"I'm sure you feel the same way. But you know who I am. I have a history here. People in town know me, and know my story. You may be my sister, but you're also a stranger. I want to see something that will prove beyond any doubt that you're Rhona. It's up to you and Frank to provide that proof, and so far neither of you has done that."

Erin stood. "I'll see you get proof, but you know what I think, Tess? I think you might have put on a good show, but you never wanted me to come back. After all, with me gone, you're the sole owner of Howard Manufacturing and this house, and all of the Howard money. You don't want me back, because then you would have to share."

She turned and stalked to the door while Tess watched her go. Is that how I look to others? Of course, she wanted Rhona back. She'd spent her life searching for her sister. But was she so out of line to want to be sure? She'd been taken advantage of before, and she didn't want that to happen again.

The phone rang. She let the answering machine take it, but there was no voice, just the sound of heavy breathing and then the click of a receiver being replaced. The hairs on her arms prickled. She'd been getting a lot of these phone calls lately, when no one said anything. They weren't as disturbing as the tapes of Rhona, but they still got on her nerves, which was probably what the caller intended.

Tess checked the doors, making sure everything was locked, and then fixed a salad and a glass of tea. There were no more phone calls, which was a relief, and after watching the evening news she forced herself to get up and turn out the lights, except for the one she left burning at night. She pulled the curtains aside a bit to look out at the yard. No one stood under the spreading branches of the old oak tree, but she stared into the darkness, looking for movement, a darker shadow, anything to show that someone lurked there. Finally she drew the curtains together and climbed the stairs to her bedroom. She sat down on the bed, listening to the silence, hating it, but afraid to turn on the radio or television, because it might mask the sounds of anyone in the house.

Nerves on edge, she buried her face in her hands and started praying. She had to depend on God to keep her safe. He was all she had, and she knew from experience that when God was all she had to hang onto, He would always be enough.

Still she lay in her bed, staring into the darkness, wondering what the night would hold.

CHAPTER EIGHTEEN

Tess put in a normal day at work, going over sales records, checking inventory, talking to the plant manager. She stopped at the deli, and bought a rotisserie chicken and some potato salad. The phone didn't ring with one of those nerve-wracking calls, or calls from anyone else. She turned on the television, but the noise made her nervous. So did the quiet, but at least she could hear if someone was sneaking up on her. She wandered from the living room to the kitchen to stand in the unlighted room, staring out the window. Nothing moved or seemed out of the ordinary. Still, she felt tension building inside her.

Finally, she made sure the alarm was set, turned out the lights, and climbed the stairs to her bedroom, wondering if she could get through the night without anything happening. Once in bed, she felt restless, had a hard time settling down, but eventually, worn out, she fell asleep.

Tess jarred awake, staring at the darkened corners of her room, nerves stressed to the max. Had something startled her, or was she just having a bad dream? She strained to hear.

Silence.

Sighing, she forced herself to relax. The alarm would alert her if anything was wrong. A faint creaking sound brought her wide-awake again. She lay rigid, listening, senses tuned.

The door to her room eased open, and she jerked to a sitting position. A dark form hurtled toward her. Tess struggled to get away, but rough hands grabbed her. A cloth clamped over her nose and mouth, cutting off the scream surging up from deep inside. Harsh fumes clogged her nostrils, stealing her breath. She tried to break free, but gradually, against her will, she sank into a bottomless pit, falling—falling—

Voices called Tess through the fog swirling in her mind. Her mouth felt like it was packed with dry cotton.

She moaned.

"She's coming to."

The words reached her, pulling her into the present. She forced her eyes open. Clyde Perkins loomed over her. She was lying on a couch in a strange room. Tess licked her lips. "Water—"

She heard water running, as if it was gushing from a faucet, and a dark-haired man with a beard shoved a glass at her. She struggled into a sitting position. Grasping the glass with both hands, she greedily gulped the lukewarm liquid until it was all gone. He took the empty container from her, placing it on a nearby table. She blinked away the remaining darkness and looked around her. The man who had brought her the water stood a short distance away. He looked to be in his late thirties, early forties. She'd never seen him before. A heavy-set woman sat in a chair on the other side of the room, watching her.

"About time you woke up."

Tess blinked at her. "Who are you?"

If she'd ever seen this woman, she would have remembered. The twisted grin, the narrowed dark eyes, the untidy white hair would have made an impression.

"You should know me. After all, you stayed with me for a week while you were four."

It couldn't be. Erin had said she was dead. This had to be an imposter. She stared at the woman, searching for something familiar. "Aggie?"

"The one and only. Welcome back. You didn't stay with me long the first time, and you won't be around long now." Aggie glanced at the two men. "Get her out of here. I couldn't stand the sight of her when she was a four-year-old whining brat, and I don't like her looks any better now."

Clyde grabbed her arm and jerked her upright. "Come along. We've got a nice place all ready for you."

Tess tried to pull away from him, but she felt weak, disoriented. He hauled her outside and around the house. She stumbled over a loose rock, almost falling. Clyde yanked her up, dragging her along behind him.

The night air revived her somewhat. She breathed in deep gulps, trying to clear her head. He stopped at a cellar door at the rear of the house, fumbling with the latch. She couldn't go in there! Tess clawed at him, trying to break his grip. He swung her around, slamming her against the doorframe. Sparks of light flickered behind her eyes. She struggled to breathe.

He jerked the door open and pushed her inside. Tess stumbled down a flight of steps, struggled to keep her balance. His hand was on her back, shoving. She sprawled on the floor, dirt and grit pricking her hands. Something soft landed on her and bounced off. The door slammed, the lock rattled.

She was alone in the dark.

Tess struggled to her feet, listening but not hearing anything. She worked her way to the steps by feeling the walls and shuffling her feet to keep from falling. When she reached the rough boards forming a door, she leaned against them, trying to think. Why had they brought her here, and what did they plan to do with her?

She sank down on the concrete step, gasping out a prayer. "Please—please help me—" The silence mocked her, but she forced her mind to focus on God. He'd help her. He had to, she didn't have anyone else.

Her thoughts turned to Neil. Would she ever see him again? These people had tried to kill him, too. Was he still in danger? She bowed her head, praying for his safety.

• • •

Neil tried to call Tess for the third time, but she still didn't answer, neither her landline nor the cell phone. Worried, he got to his feet and went out to the car. He'd drive to her place and see if she was all right. When he reached the house, her car was parked in the driveway. He climbed the steps to the front door and rang the doorbell.

No answer.

He tried again. Frustrated, he grabbed the doorknob, feeling it turn beneath his hand. He paused. Why wasn't her door locked? Slowly, he pushed it open, waiting for the alarm to go off. Nothing happened.

"Tess?"

Nothing, just silence thick and frightening. He eased back and walked out to his car.

Burke answered the phone and listened while Neil told him what he suspected. "We'll be right there. You wait outside."

Neil walked back to the porch, afraid of what they would find. Every instinct urged him to go inside, run through the rooms looking for her, but knowing he might destroy valuable evidence, he forced himself to wait.

A few minutes later, a police car pulled into the drive and Burke got out. "Okay, let's see what's wrong." He pushed the door open and stepped inside, pausing to look around. "I thought she had an alarm."

"She does, but it's not working."

"I see. Well, let's take a look. You stay behind me. Don't go wandering off on your own. I'm stretching it to let you come inside, but since you were a cop once, you know what to do."

They walked through the downstairs, finding nothing. Burke led the way up the stairs, stopping to point at a smear of dried mud on one of the steps. He checked every room, Neil right behind him. They paused at the door of the largest bedroom. The bedclothes were rumpled, the small bedside rug wadded up and kicked aside. Burke pulled out his cell phone and started punching in numbers.

Neil listened as Burke requested a team to come investigate. He felt sick. Why hadn't he insisted, in spite of her protests, that she leave this house? Or force her to let someone stay with her? But he had a feeling nothing he could have done would have prevented this. Someone had been determined to get to Tess. They just had to bide their time and grab her when no one else was around.

They went back downstairs and out the front door. Burke leaned against a porch post, and Neil slumped in a chair, just waiting. *God, keep her safe, and help me find her. Show me what to do.*

Another police car pulled in and parked behind Burke's cruiser. Neil waited while the investigators went inside and looked around. After a while, Burke came back out. "Someone messed with the alarm, fixing it so it wouldn't go off. Clipped the wires."

Neil nodded. He'd already figured that out.

Burke took a deep breath, and stared out at the street. "We're going to do all we can to find her."

Neil nodded, knowing while Burke meant it, they didn't have much to go on. The police finally left, and Neil drove back to his office to sit at his desk, his thoughts churning. The door opened, and Bob came in with Maxine. Neil glared at them. Whatever they had in mind, he didn't want to hear it. He needed to focus on Tess.

Bob motioned for Maxine to sit down, and then took the chair next to her. "I know you don't want to talk right now, but you need to hear what she has to say."

Maxine looked at him and drew in a deep breath, exhaling gently before she started talking. "I'm not Maxine Crowley. I'm *Rhona Howard*."

Neil shot Bob a look. Not another one. "You got any way to prove that?"

Rhona spoke first. "Yes, DNA will prove it. But right now we need to concentrate on finding my sister. I'm sure Aggie Clark and Clyde Perkins have Tess."

"So are you part of the plan?" There had to be a reason why she turned up at the same time they did.

"No. They intended to use Erin to pass for me and collect the heritance after they killed Tess. When I found out about it I ran away."

"Why didn't you go to the police?"

"I was afraid to. I thought I could watch them, try to stop them without giving myself away. If they knew I was in town, I'd be dead by now. I've had twenty-four years of living with their abuse. It did something to me, destroyed me as a person. I thought you and the police would protect Tess." She wiped tears. "I'm so ashamed. I put my own safety ahead of my sister's. But I'll do everything I can to help her now."

Neil stared at her, not missing the way Bob was nodding. Bob would be hard to fool. "Are you the one who called wanting me to go to the park?"

Maxine shook her head, "No, that was probably Aggie."

"Why would she want to involve me?" That was the part that didn't make sense. He didn't have any connection with the Howard family. Or he didn't until he met Tess.

Maxine stared at him. "You really don't know? It's because of Lester."

Neil stared at her, trying to make sense of this. "Lester? Lester who?"

"Lester Holt, Aggie's son from her first marriage. He's in prison. You sent him there. He was one of the men who killed Rebecca White."

Neil froze, the breath leaving his body. Sure, he remembered Lester Holt. He remembered the names of every man who had a hand in Rebecca's death. He'd never forget them, never forget their faces.

Maxine's expression turned compassionate. "That's right. Aggie's son helped kill Rebecca. He's in prison for life, and Aggie hates you with a passion. You were supposed to die that night at the park. So was Tess."

Neil heaved a breath, adjusting to this information. How about that for irony? He'd moved from New York City to a remote corner of the Ozarks, hoping to run from what had happened there, and he'd ended up in Lester Holt's hometown. God must have a wicked sense of humor to have allowed this to happen.

He looked from her to Bob and then back again. "If they have Tess, where can they be holding her?"

"I don't know. They had a farm—I think it was Aggie's family farm—not far from here. That's where they held us until the ransom was paid. It was dark the night they brought us, and I only saw it from the outside the day we left. I've never been back since then."

Bob spoke for the first time since Maxine—Rhona— had started talking. "We need to talk to the police, tell them what we know. Maybe they would have some idea where this place is."

Neil had come to accept Maxine was who she said she was. She knew too much to be a fake. He picked up the phone and started dialing. After he explained to Burke what had happened, he promised they would come to the police station right away. When he hung up the phone, Bob and Rhona were on their feet, ready to go. He locked the door and motioned them toward his SUV. "I'll drive."

They climbed in without protesting, and Neil drove the short distance to the police station. No one spoke, which suited him just fine. He had a lot to think about. Now that he'd lost her, he realized fully just how much Tess meant to him. With God's help, he would do everything in his power to find her.

Lester Holt.

The sniveling, would-be tough guy, who had helped kill an unarmed woman. Neil didn't know what Burke planned to do, but he meant to be in on it.

They sat down across the desk from Burke. Stanley and a couple of other policemen were there, too. Rhona told her story again, and Burke glanced from Neil to Bob. "You guys believe she's who she says?"

Bob nodded. "I'd trust her with my life. I know her, and I'd believe anything she told me."

Rhona turned and smiled at him, and in that instant Neil decided she was telling the truth. There was no mistaking her expression. She loved the guy, and from the sappy way Bob stared at her, he was hooked.

Neil turned his attention back to Burke. "What are we going to do now?"

Burke glanced at the other policemen and shrugged. "Now, we're going to do all we can to find this place. I appreciate you coming to us with this. We've got to get to work. If you learn anything else, be sure you let us know."

He stood, and Neil took the hint, standing too. Rhona and Bob followed him outside. They drove back to the office and got out.

Rhona's lips quivered. "If you hear anything let me know, please."

"And if you think of anything that would help, I want to hear it." The words came out more harshly than Neil intended, but he was scared. These people had tried to kill Tess several times. What would stop them now?

Rhona nodded, and Bob slid his arm around her waist. "Don't worry. We'll be in touch. We've got to find her as soon as we can."

They got in Bob's car and drove away, and Neil stood in front of his office, not sure what to do next. Tess? Where are you? Stay alive until I get there. Wherever you are, I'll find you. He would keep that promise whatever it took.

Neil went inside to sit staring at the wall, numb and lost, praying for help. He wanted to get in his car and drive until he found her, but that would be a fool's game. A total waste of time, since he had no idea where to look. He turned to the computer and brought up a map of Cedar City and the surrounding area. He started checking off the farms, making a list of the people who owned them. Probably the police were doing the same thing, but he had to do something. Tess needed him. Failure wasn't an option. Not this time.

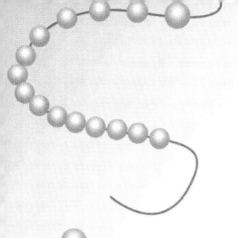

CHAPTER NINETEEN

The next morning Neil was back at the computer. He hadn't slept much last night, worrying about Tess. He'd identified most of the owners of area farms, although there were a few for which he hadn't been able to find names. He planned to take the list to Burke, and see if it was something useful. Probably not, but working it out gave him the illusion he was doing something helpful.

The door opened, and Bob stepped in. One look at him, and Neil knew something was wrong. Bob blurted out, "Rhona has disappeared. She didn't show up at work, and she's not home. It's just like it was with Tess."

Neil's heart thudded. "Where does she live?"

"In an apartment a few blocks from me. I moved her there because I didn't think it was safe where she was staying." Bob stood by the door, looking ready to bolt out.

Neil stared at him, trying to take it in. That meant both of the Howard girls were missing, and someone had plans to kill them. This was major trouble. "Have you been to the police?"

"I'm going right now. I want you to go with me. We both have a stake in this."

"Right." Neil got to his feet and started for the door. "Let's go."

This time Bob drove—a mistake on Neil's part. He ran the town's only red light, not even bothering to slow down. Neil breathed a sigh of relief when they pulled up in front of the police station. Bob beat him to the door by three feet.

Burke raised his eyebrows when they walked in. "What's wrong now?"

Bob leaned over the desk, resting his hands on the wooden top. "It's Rhona. She's gone."

Burke stared at him. "You serious?"

"Yeah, I'm serious. I can't find her. She didn't go to work this morning, and she's not at her house. Her car's there, just like with Tess."

"Ah-huh. Okay, how sure are you that she's Rhona Howard?"

"I'm positive. Why?"

"Then I wonder who the woman is who got in touch with Frank Walpin."

Neil rocked to a stop. Well, yes, exactly who was this Erin, and what did she have to do with Tess and Rhona disappearing? Tess and Rhona. This was a rerun of what had happened when they were children, and this time the results might be more deadly.

●　●　●

Tess sat on an overturned large, square, metal pan in the gloomy cellar. Light seeped in around the boards covering the one small window, and she could glimpse a faint glow of sunlight. She'd found some of her clothes on the floor, along with a pair of canvas slippers. Apparently that was what Clyde had thrown last night. At least it was better than the nightgown she'd been wearing when she was snatched from her bed.

A rattle of the latch sent her surging to her feet. She reached the foot of the steps just as the door swung open and someone was propelled inside. The newcomer stumbled down the steps, and Tess reached out to catch her. "Maxine? What are you doing here?"

Maxine steadied herself by putting one hand against the wall. "I'm here for the same reason you're here. We're sisters. I'm Rhona Howard."

Tess backed up a step, stunned. "What?"

Maxine straightened, and pushed away from the wall. "I am Rhona Howard."

Tess let the disbelief show in her voice. "You can prove it?"

Maxine stepped past her, moving into the body of the cellar. "As a matter of fact, I can. DNA will remove all doubt, if we get out of here alive, but I have something more personal. You had a doll, a baby doll that could talk. I had one, too. You got mad at me and broke mine, and I dropped yours out of the window in our room just to get even."

Tess laughed out loud. "I hated you for days."

"I think we both got a spanking over that. And do you remember the Elkins Grocery Store, how we went in and charged a bunch of candy? We made ourselves sick gorging on it."

"And we were grounded, not allowed to leave the yard." This really was her sister. No one else could know the childish pranks they had gotten into.

Joy flooded through Tess. Her sister had come home.

Rhona was smiling now. "And we got into Mom's makeup. We looked like clowns."

Tears rolled down Tess's cheeks. "I've missed you so much. Thank God you're here."

Suddenly they were in each other's arms, laughing and crying at the same time. This was the reunion she had hoped for.

They drew apart, and Rhona patted Tess's cheek. "Oh, Tessie, I've dreamed about this for years. It's just exactly what I hoped for."

Tessie. The childhood name only her sister had called her. "Me too. It's so good to have you back. But where have you been all this time?"

Rhona sat down on the lower step, and motioned toward the upturned pan. "Let's sit down and talk, and then we'll make plans for getting out of here alive."

Tess dropped down on the metal seat and waited. Rhona drew a deep breath and started talking. "I was with Morris and Aggie until he was arrested, and then with Aggie and Clyde. I know you wonder why I didn't call, but I couldn't. At first they told me that my parents didn't want me. I was treated like their daughter, until I got older and Erin came to stay, and then I lived in a room in the attic. I wasn't allowed to use the phone, wasn't allowed to go to school. Aggie homeschooled me for a while. Finally, I ended up living in a little shed in the backyard, in a pen with high walls and a lock on the gate."

Tess stared at her in dismay. She'd never imagined Rhona was living under such terrible conditions. "Erin? You know Erin? She claimed to be you."

Rhona smiled and shrugged. "Yes, I know Erin. She's Aggie's niece. Her parents are dead, and Aggie took her in. Her real name is Erin Wheeler. By the time she came along, I was ten years old, and Aggie had gotten tired of me. With Erin to raise, she didn't need me."

"Wheeler? Neil was looking for a Ralph Wheeler who was supposed to be missing."

Rhona laughed. "He's not missing—he's been at Aggie's, helping plan this caper. I guess he forget to let Coletta in on what he was doing. He's that dark-haired guy upstairs. He and Clyde have been working together trying to get rid of you."

Tess asked the question that had been bothering her. "Did they bring you to Cedar City with them?"

"No, I heard them talking. They were going to pass Erin off as me, and when they had established her credentials, they planned to kill you. So I escaped and ran away."

Tess stared at her, thinking about this. "If you escaped, then why couldn't you get away before?"

"We had a neighbor woman whose backyard connected with ours. She saw me out there. Sometimes at night, after everyone had gone to bed, she would come out and talk to me. She wanted to call the police, but I was afraid if she did, and Aggie and Morris found out who was responsible, they would kill her. She was the only friend I had. When I told her what they were planning, she got her son to bring a ladder and help me over the fence. She cut my hair, changed the color, taught me to apply makeup, bought me new clothes and a bus ticket. I arrived, got a job, and started looking the situation over."

"Why didn't you tell me who you were?"

Rhona reached out and took Tess's hand in both of hers. "I wanted to protect you until I had learned what was going on. If they knew I was in town, I wouldn't have had a chance. They would have killed me, and dumped my body someplace where it couldn't be found. Make no mistake. They are very dangerous, and they don't care about anyone."

Tess glanced around the cellar that was their prison. "So what do we do now?"

Rhona got to her feet. "Now we figure out how to get out of here. I've been their prisoner for twenty-four years. I'm ready to fight back."

●   ●   ●

Neil and Bob huddled around a table at the police station with Burke and Stanley, trying to determine where the two women could be. Neil stabbed the table with a forefinger, yielding to frustration. "They have to be held somewhere fairly close."

Bob nodded. "Probably in the same house they were held in when they were kids. According to Rhona, it was in this area, but we have no idea who owned it."

The four men looked at each other, and Neil asked, "Was there anyplace around here where Morris and Aggie Clark lived?"

Stanley shook his head. "I never knew them, if they did."

"Morris is in jail," Neil said, thinking out loud. "Rhona said Aggie was married to someone named Holt. They had a son."

"Holt?" Stanley interrupted. "Wait a minute. Aggie Walpin. She married Dick Holt. He died. Had pneumonia, I think?"

"Walpin?" Neil asked. "As in Frank Walpin?"

"Yeah, I think she's Frank's aunt or something. The old Walpin place is down the road from mine. No one lives there now. It's kind of run down."

"Tess and I drove by there the other day. There were a couple of cars out in the driveway." Neil rose to his feet. Bob shoved his chair back and stood.

Burke gave them a stern look. "Where do you think you're going?"

Neil answered for them both. "We're going to check it out."

Burke got to his feet. "You two stay out of this. I'm going out there, and taking Stanley with me. I'm calling in a couple of other cars to meet us there."

Neil matched him stare for stare. "You can go first, but we're going to follow you." No way was he giving in on this. Tess needed him, and he wasn't about to let her down.

After a moment, Burke nodded. "All right, but you get in my way, and I'll arrest you for interfering with a police action."

He gave instructions to the dispatcher to send men to pick up Frank Walpin and Erin. "I figure they're both involved. Better be safe than sorry. I want them where they can't run. Now, let's get going."

They ripped past Stanley's place, sirens blaring. The next house would be the old Walpin place. Bob had his head bowed, praying, and Neil sent a petition up, too, while concentrating on his driving. They needed all the help they could get.

• • •

Rhona and Tess had given up on the window, and were trying to break through the door. Tess hooked her fingers through a crack where the wood seemed rotten enough to tear. With Rhona's help, she managed to rip off a piece, leaving a hole big enough to stick her hand through. After fumbling around for a minute, she found the lock, which turned out to be a metal fastener that fit over a loop, with a teaspoon inserted through to hold it. She pulled out the spoon, and swung the door open.

Tess blinked in the bright sunlight after the dimness of the old cellar, but nothing could disguise the hefty figures of Clyde Perkins and Ralph Wheeler standing there, watching them. Clyde grabbed Tess, and Ralph caught Rhona and pulled her out into the open. Clyde forced Tess around the house, up the steps, and into the living room. Ralph shoved Rhona in behind them and closed the door. Aggie was sitting in a chair, watching. The men pushed Rhona and Tess down on the old couch, raising a cloud of dust.

Aggie glared at them. "I ought to have killed both of you when I had the chance. You've been nothing but trouble." She glanced at Clyde. "I can't think of any reason to keep them alive, can you?"

He grinned. "I'm thinking hard, but nothing occurs to me."

A wail of sirens sounded in the distance, drawing closer. Clyde and Ralph whirled, running to the door as police cars pulled into the yard. The men each held a gun. They slid outside, sheltered from view by the thick autumn clematis vines climbing the porch posts. The sirens fell silent.

Tess dived across the space separating her from Aggie, aware that Rhona was right behind her. She grabbed the older woman by the front of her shirt. Rhona gripped her right arm. Together they pulled Aggie out of her chair to crash against the floor. Tess straddled her back, holding her down.

"Get off me," Aggie screeched "Clyde! Help!"

Tess tangled her fingers in Aggie's frowsy white hair. "Don't you dare fight me. I've got twenty-four years to get even for, so don't even think of giving me a reason to hurt you."

"And that goes double for me," Rhona said. "Payday's been a long time coming."

She got up and raced across the room, slamming the door and locking it so the men couldn't come back inside.

Tess twisted around so she could look out of the window. The police were fanning out, yelling directions. She saw Neil and Bob crouching behind a car, and her heart stopped as Clyde stood up and raised his gun. A shot rang out, and he dropped to the porch floor. Ralph tossed his gun aside and raised his arms.

The police approached, weapons drawn. When they reached the porch, Rhona unlocked the door so they could come in. Neil shoved his way past Burke, rushing across the cracked linoleum to reach Tess. Two policemen followed him, hauled Aggie to her feet, and led her outside.

Tess saw Bob and Rhona locked in an embrace, and then Neil's arms were around her, holding her so tight against him she could feel his heartbeat. He smoothed her hair back from her face, his voice trembling. "I thought I had lost you. Thank God you're safe."

She clung to him, giving him a tremulous smile. "It looks like you've rescued me again."

He caressed her cheek. "I know this probably isn't the time, but we need to talk. I loved Rebecca, but she belongs to the past. I'm looking forward to the future, and I hope you'll want to share it with me. I love you, Tess. If you'll have me, I want to spend the rest of our lives together."

She smiled up at him, blinking back tears. "I love you, too, and together sounds wonderful."

His lips met hers, and she knew the chains that had bound her to the past had been broken forever. Before her stretched a new life, a life with the man she loved. Her sister was home, she had kept her promise to her parents, and she had Neil and the love she'd never expected.

God was definitely in His heaven, and after twenty-four miserable years, all was finally right with her world.

Acknowledgements

Special thanks to Terry Burns for being such a great agent. Thanks also to Meaghan Burnett from Elance for being so easy to work with and to Eddie Jones at Lighthouse Publishing of the Carolina's for believing in me and in this book. I also want to thank Elizabeth Easter for her great editing, and a special thank you to my private critique group: Mary Lowe, Carol Parscale, Ronica Stramel, Randi Perry and Alice Leverich. You all do a great job. I appreciate you more than words can say."

Made in the USA
Las Vegas, NV
10 March 2021